Redeeming Honor

I0610073

E.A. West

Redeeming Honor
COPYRIGHT 2017 by Elizabeth West

Contact Information: titleadmin@pelicanbookgroup.com

Cover Art by *Nicola Martinez*

White Rose Publishing, a division of Pelican Ventures, LLC
www.pelicanbookgroup.com PO Box 1738 *Aztec, NM * 87410

White Rose Publishing Circle and Rosebud logo is a trademark of Pelican Ventures, LLC

Publishing History
First White Rose Edition, 2017
Paperback Edition ISBN 978-1-5223-0001-4
Electronic Edition ISBN 978-1-5223-0000-7
Published in the United States of America

Dedication

To the brave interpreters who have risked everything
to help make the world a safer place.

What People are Saying

"Books such as Healing in Haven Falls are a rare jewel to treasure."

~ Suzie Housley, Romance Junkies

The Key to Charlotte
"This is an incredibly sweet romance, profound and absolutely unforgettable—a bite-sized read that packs a super-sized emotional wallop."

~ Delia Latham, inspirational romance author

"I highly recommend The Key to Charlotte to anyone who needs to be reminded of the love available to us through both other humans and God."

~ Crystal, CK2S Kwips and Kritiques

Breath of Christmas
"There is something so beautiful about the way EA West creates her stories. They tug on the heart, they depict realistic characters, and I love the unique circumstances and fresh plots she develops."

~ Marianne Evans, inspirational romance author

Bogota Blessings
"This novel contains a nice melding of cultures by combining both the mainstream American citizen and a Columbian. Overall, a well-done romance and an inspiring read!"

~ Shaunna Gonzales, InD'tale Magazine

1

Meghan Carpenter glanced up from the spinning wheel as her twin brother stepped into her workshop, cellphone in hand. He dropped onto the wooden bench by the wall and watched her spin a few more inches of roving into worsted weight yarn. Ever since Ryan moved in after his discharge from the Marine Corps, he got quiet at odd moments or seemed fascinated by mundane things, such as her spinning yarn for about the millionth time. This time, however, she sensed he had something on his mind he wanted to share.

After waiting without success for him to speak, she stopped working altogether and studied him. "What's up?"

"I just got off the phone with one of the guys I served with in Afghanistan." He sighed and laid his cellphone beside him. Then he leaned forward and braced his arms on his knees. "He's had it rough, got injured in a blast, but he's recovered to the point he no longer needs rehabilitation."

"That's great news, right?" Something wasn't adding up about her brother's demeanor and his words. "So, why do you look so worried?"

"He doesn't have anywhere to go. Ever since he got to the States, he's been living in hospitals or apartments for patients receiving long-term therapies. Since he doesn't need treatment anymore, he's got to leave. Problem is, he doesn't have any family to take him in and he's not quite ready to search for a job yet."

"Kind of like you." Meghan adjusted her work so it wouldn't untwist and rose from her stool to sit by her brother. She laid a hand on his shoulder, her heart going out to him and his unnamed friend. With as much trouble as Ryan had adjusting to civilian life with family to support him, she couldn't imagine how much more difficult it was for his friend. "Do you have any ideas for how you can help him?"

He slid a glance her way, reminding her of when they were kids and he wanted her to do something. "Well, you've got that other guest room upstairs, and I'm sure my friend would be willing to help out around here the same way I do. So…"

"You want to bring him here?" The nudge in her heart encouraged her to go along with her brother's plan, but she didn't know which of the men he'd served with she would be taking in. Not all of them were men she trusted under her roof.

"Yeah. He's a good man. A strong Christian." Ryan turned toward her, his eyes pleading as he spoke. "I really think you'll like him, Megs. And your farm would be good for him. He needs a safe place to adjust to life in the States."

Again, like her brother. She bit her lip, praying for wisdom. Once more, her heart nudged her to listen to Ryan and let his friend live on her small Indiana farm. "OK. He can stay here. When will he be moving in?"

"He's just a few hours from here, so I could leave early tomorrow to pick him up and have him back here by around suppertime."

"That soon?"

"Yeah. Apparently, he's already stayed in his apartment longer than they originally intended, but he didn't tell me he didn't have anywhere to go until he called a little while ago." Ryan leaned over and wrapped her in a hug. "Thanks, Megs. I know he'll appreciate you letting him stay here as much as I do."

He grabbed his cellphone and left the workshop as he dialed.

Meghan moved back to her spinning wheel, but she didn't resume her work. Instead, her mind spun with what had just happened. This morning she had wondered again how long it would take her brother to recover from whatever he had endured during five tours in Afghanistan. Now, she faced the reality of having two recovering marines living under her roof. While she appreciated the help with her huge garden and herd of alpacas, her brother wasn't always easy to live with. He'd improved in the four months since he moved in, but he still prowled through the house in the middle of the night sometimes. When out in the fields he often took on the "thousand-yard stare."

Hopefully, his friend would have an easier time than her brother had adjusting to normal, boring life, but the way Ryan had spoken about him indicated he might be in worse shape.

Thank You, Lord, for blessing me with patience.

Meghan rose from her stool and headed into the main part of the house. If she was going to have another long-term houseguest arrive tomorrow, she needed to make sure the guestroom was ready. Fresh linens on the bed, maybe a friendly houseplant on the windowsill, and a quick dusting and vacuuming would take care of most of the preparations. She also needed to make sure the closet and dresser were empty.

As she placed her foot on the bottom step, Ryan

came down the hall from the kitchen. "Hey, change of plans. I'm leaving now, and we'll be here in time for lunch tomorrow."

"Why the change?" She lowered her foot to the floor and faced him.

"He needs help packing up the rest of his stuff." Ryan grinned and walked toward the front door, calling over his shoulder, "Don't worry. He really doesn't have a lot. See you tomorrow!"

Meghan stared at the door long after he closed it. Her brother left in a better mood than she'd seen in a long time. Could he need his friend to live with them as much as, if not more than, his friend needed a place to stay?

~*~

The oven timer dinged, and Meghan grabbed a hot pad. Golden-brown cookies filled the air with the delicious scents of vanilla and chocolate. She set the tray on the granite counter, shut off the oven, and then turned to the task of transferring chocolate chip cookies to the cooling rack.

As she set the baking sheet in the sink, the front door opened. Meghan's heart jumped, and she hurried from the kitchen, eager to see which of Ryan's friends would be living in her house. She stepped into the hall and spotted her brother and a swarthy-skinned, black-haired man wearing huge dark sunglasses. Each of them carried a black suitcase.

Ryan grinned as his friend closed the door. "Hey, Meghan, this is my buddy Basir Hamidi. Basir, meet my sister, Meghan."

The black-haired man removed his sunglasses to

reveal a pair of wire-rimmed glasses and scar tissue around his tawny-brown eyes. "Thank you for letting me stay in your home."

Meghan swallowed her surprise at his heavy accent and pushed aside her sorrow that he had endured something terrible to cause the scars. Regardless of what he had been through, the only thing that should matter to her was helping him to feel comfortable in her home. She offered a warm smile and clasped her hands at her waist. "I'm glad I had an empty guestroom for you. I'll let Ryan give you the grand tour of the place while I put the finishing touches on lunch, but remember that this is your home, too, for however long you need it."

"Thank you." He inclined his head, his right hand over his heart. Then, he lowered his hand and glanced at Ryan.

Her brother slung an arm around Basir's shoulders and guided him to the stairs. "Your room's up here."

Meghan returned to the kitchen and struggled to wrap her mind around her new houseguest. She'd expected an American marine, but her brother had brought home an Afghan man. Had Basir somehow become a marine? Had he been part of the Afghan army? Questions flowed in a steady stream as she chopped hardboiled eggs for the chef's salads she'd planned.

She paused in the middle of scooping them into a bowl. Did Basir have any food preferences that would make her planned lunch a bad idea? Her gaze strayed to the refrigerator, where a bowl of ham cubes waited for her brother's salad. Since Afghanistan was a Muslim country and Islam forbade the consumption of pork, would Basir mind her serving a pork product?

Ryan had said he was a Christian, but she had no idea how much of the Islamic religious mores might have become part of Afghan culture.

Too late now to change the lunch menu. She would just have to hope he overlooked any foods he couldn't eat for cultural reasons and forgave her ignorance. At least she also had a bowl of smoked turkey cubes for the salads. Before she prepared supper, however, she would be sure to ask about any preferences or dietary restrictions Basir might have.

She set the dishes of toppings on the table, along with a huge bowl of green salad. A sense of accomplishment filled her as she gazed at the lunch that had mostly come from her own property. She had grown the lettuces, carrots, peppers, cucumbers, onions, and tomatoes. The only ingredients she had bought were the dressing, meats, and cheeses. She had traded a neighbor produce for the eggs.

The men entered as she poured the last glass of iced tea and placed it on the table. She set the pitcher on the counter and joined her brother and his friend at the table.

"Looks good, Megs," Ryan said as he settled into his seat. He indicated a chair to Basir, who then pulled it out and sat down.

"Thanks." She took a seat, noticing how easily her brother and his friend interacted. There were little things that indicated her brother must have learned quite a bit about Afghan culture, such as indicating Basir's seat, but Basir also seemed comfortable in an American kitchen. Maybe it didn't matter whether certain foods were taboo in Afghanistan. If he had been in the United States long enough to adapt to the American way of life, he might not stick to Afghan culture any longer. With that thought in mind, she decided to quit making assumptions about her new houseguest and treat him the same way she would treat anyone else.

The three of them bowed their heads, and Ryan thanked God for the meal and Basir's safe arrival. As they passed around the dishes, Meghan noticed Basir never used his left hand to touch the serving utensils, only his right hand. He also bypassed the ham, which didn't mean much since she didn't take any either.

She couldn't contain her curiosity any longer. "So, Basir, Ryan tells me you guys served together in Afghanistan."

"Yes, I was an interpreter." He shifted in his seat and glanced at Ryan.

Ryan grinned and waved his empty fork toward Basir. "Don't let him fool you. He's the best interpreter I ever worked with. He was also a lot more fun than some of the others we had."

A faint smile lifted the corners of Basir's mouth. "You taught me much American culture during those times."

"Hey, I owed it to you after all you taught me about Afghan culture in the course of doing your job." Ryan shifted his attention to Meghan. "I always told him he should be a teacher somewhere, because he's great at sharing information in a way that's easy to understand."

"Only about the way things are done in Afghanistan." Basir dropped his gaze to his plate, apparently intent on studying the piece of cucumber he poked with his fork.

"Eh, that's beside the point." Ryan speared a ham chunk. "So, are you ready to learn how to be an alpaca farmer?"

Basir lifted his head, interest shining in his eyes. "Is it very different from being a sheep farmer?"

Ryan opened his mouth, but Meghan spoke first. "Not really. We have to take good care of the animals and shear them when their wool is ready. Did you live on a sheep farm before you became an interpreter?"

"My grandfather raised sheep." Basir sighed. "He always said I would take over when he grew too old, but that was not to be. Now a cousin owns the farm."

"Is it because of your injuries?" Her heart went out to him at the thought he might not be able to do farm work because of getting wounded. If that was the case, she would find ways for him to help out that weren't physically taxing.

"No, it is because I chose to help the Americans."

Confusion filled her, and she looked to her brother. "I don't understand."

Ryan took a sip of his tea before speaking. "It's hard to explain exactly what happened, but basically his family disowned him to protect themselves from the Taliban."

"Oh, that's so sad." Meghan blinked back tears and turned to Basir, who silently moved the food around his plate. "Basir, as long as you're here, we'll be your family. I know it's not the same, but…"

He briefly met her gaze. "Ryan has been like a brother to me since we first worked together. It is an honor to be included in your family."

Ryan moved the conversation on to the farm and his work on it. Basir seemed comfortable with the topic of farming, but Meghan only half-listened to the men talk. How could she help Basir heal not only from his time working with the American military, but also from the loss of his family?

~*~

Basir sat on the foot of the bed and stared at the multicolored oval rug covering the center of the wood floor. He had known for years that Afghanistan was a poor country. His family, although better off than many in the area, had struggled to survive. But he had never really understood just how poor they were until he came to America. Even his time working with the American military hadn't prepared him for the shock of going from small mud-walled houses with dirt floors to this large two-story house with polished wood floors, rugs, and smooth walls painted in light colors.

The most difficult part for him to grasp was that Meghan, a young unmarried woman, owned the house, land, buildings, and animals surrounding it. Ryan said she hadn't inherited it from a family member. She had saved and bought it for herself. And yet, according to Ryan, she wasn't wealthy.

"America is a strange place," Basir muttered for what felt like the thousandth time since leaving his homeland.

A pair of taps brought his gaze to the open door. Ryan stood in the doorway, a look of inquiry on his face. "You ready to see the farm and meet the animals?"

"Yes." Basir stood and grabbed his baseball cap from the dresser. Then, he picked up his sunglasses and met Ryan's gaze with a sigh. "I hate these things."

"I know, but your eyes are too light sensitive to get rid of them."

"I just wish I didn't have to choose between hiding my eyes and suffering searing pain." Basir sighed again and followed Ryan out of the room. "Thankfully, the doctors think I will not need them forever. Only until my eyes finish healing and adjust to the damage that was done."

Ryan clapped a hand to his shoulder as they headed for the stairs. "Then you can look forward to the day you no longer need them."

"If only I could look forward to the day I would no longer have migraines, but the doctors tell me I will always have them because of the traumatic brain injury."

"But there is a chance they'll become less frequent, right?"

"There is a chance, yes. At least I no longer have them every day."

"We'll just have to pray for your continued healing."

"Thank you, my friend." Basir turned at the top of the stairs and placed his right hand over his heart to show his sincerity.

"No need to thank me," Ryan said with a grin. "I've been praying for you since I heard you got injured. It'd be wrong to quit now just because you're out of the hospital."

"Perhaps." He started down the stairs, and the sight of Meghan waiting in the hall below took his mind off his problems.

When Ryan had first mentioned his twin sister one day in Afghanistan, Basir had halfway expected her to look like a female version of the marine. Then, Ryan showed him a photograph, and Basir had been blown away. Although Meghan and Ryan both had brown hair and green eyes, the similarities ended there. Where Ryan was tall and solid muscle, Meghan was petite with just enough curves to attract the attention of any breathing male. She wore her hair long, almost to her waist. Today she had it pulled back in a single braid down her back, but Basir vividly remembered the soft waves it had in Ryan's photo.

She gave him a warm smile and then glanced past him to include her brother in it as they reached the bottom of the stairs. "So, are you guys helping with chores or just checking the place out this afternoon?"

"We will help you," Basir said without checking for confirmation from Ryan. Although Meghan owned the farm and apparently ran it well, he couldn't shake a sense of guilt at the thought of leaving her to do all the heavy labor. Where he came from, men did the farming while the women took care of the house and children.

Her eyes lit up, and he had to force himself not to stare. He shouldn't even be looking at her this much, but despite his best efforts, her beauty kept drawing his gaze.

"Awesome," Meghan said, her sweet voice more than making up for her flat American accent. "Let's go."

She led the way through the house to the back door, and Ryan fell into step with Basir. "You're in a hurry to get started working."

Basir shrugged, regretting answering Meghan so quickly. He should have realized her brother would pick up on it and question him about it. Showing interest in her so soon was a bad idea. Ryan didn't know how much Basir had wanted to meet her since he first saw her picture. Besides, Basir had nothing to offer her. He had no home, no family, no job. Even his honor had been destroyed by his work with the Americans and his inability to protect the people closest to him from retaliation by the Taliban. Ryan would never approve of him as a suitor for his sister.

Ryan slung an arm across his shoulders, bringing him out of his thoughts. "Yeah, I'd be in a hurry to do something too, if I had just spent the last several months in hospitals and physical therapy. All that sitting around and doing the same exercises over and over has to get boring real fast."

"I kind of liked it," Basir said, aware of Meghan listening as they passed through the kitchen. "The security, not being shot at, sleeping in a comfortable bed every night...it was almost like a vacation."

Meghan opened the back door but paused before going out. She turned toward them, her gaze clouded with concern. "Was it really so bad over there that getting injured and spending months recovering is pleasant?"

Basir glanced at Ryan, who lowered his arm and gave a small nod. Clearly, he expected Basir to be honest with her, but he didn't want to tell her too much. Part of his job as a man was to protect women, and in this case it meant telling her as little as possible about the terrible realities of his time helping the Americans.

He glanced at her and found her waiting expectantly. "Maybe for Ryan it was not so bad. But for me...yes, all the time recovering from my injuries was pleasant compared to what I endured before getting injured."

"Wow." Meghan stepped forward and before he realized what she planned, she laid her hand on his forearm. "Basir, I'm sure you must miss Afghanistan, but if it was that bad for you there, I am so glad you're here instead."

His breath caught in his throat as she gave his arm a quick rub and went out the back door. Her sympathy warmed him almost as much as her touch, but the memory of the pressure of her hand wouldn't let him go. He turned to Ryan, hoping for some insight.

"She touched me."

Ryan chuckled and nodded. "Yes, she did."

"But she's not related to me."

"That doesn't matter here." Ryan put a hand on Basir's shoulder and guided him toward the door. "American culture is different, remember? What Meghan did is show you sympathy for what you've been through and let you know she cares. While she normally wouldn't show it through touch for a stranger, she knows you're a good friend of mine."

"And that makes a difference?" Basir struggled to remember everything he had learned about American culture during his time as an interpreter and since coming to America.

"To her, yes. She knows you're trustworthy because I wouldn't have asked about you staying here if you weren't." Ryan patted him on the back and grinned. "She also knows you wouldn't dare do anything to hurt her because you'd have to deal with me if you tried it."

Basir nodded and followed his friend to where Meghan waited beside a large plot of vegetables. With no more time to talk without Meghan hearing, he could only hope Ryan knew he wouldn't dream of hurting her or any other woman. After all the time they had spent together, after all the talking they had done during downtime, surely he knew Basir well enough to trust him with his sister.

Then again, maybe knowing him so well was the issue. Could it be Ryan had already figured out that Basir was attracted to Meghan? More importantly, would he approve?

2

Two days of watching Basir and her brother interact, and Meghan still didn't know much about the Afghan man now living in her house. At first, she'd thought he was abnormally shy, but then Ryan had explained that an unmarried man speaking with an unmarried woman at length just wasn't done in Afghanistan. With that bit of knowledge tucked away in her mind, Meghan began to look for other clues about Basir's culture. He fascinated her, and she couldn't deny a budding attraction to him. What woman wouldn't be attracted to a handsome man who showed her respect at all times?

All she'd managed to learn about Basir in the two days since he moved in was that he was as close to Ryan as a brother, he went out of his way to avoid being alone in a room with her, and he watched her when he thought no one was looking. That last bit was cute, the way he would suddenly feign interest in the walls or the sky whenever she glanced in his direction. And if Ryan happened to look over, the most adorable guilty look flashed across Basir's face before he said something completely mundane to her brother.

Still, she hoped he would relax and adapt to life in America soon. Although fascinated by his foreign upbringing shining through so strongly, she wanted to talk to him without worrying she had crossed some cultural line she didn't know existed. When she laid her hand on Basir's arm his first day there, she'd thought she was offering comfort. Then, Ryan had talked to her that evening outside of Basir's hearing and explained that a woman touching a man, especially one she wasn't related to, was taboo in Afghanistan. While it explained Basir's shocked expression, she hated knowing she had made him uncomfortable by behaving in a way considered disreputable in his homeland.

So now she observed quietly, hoping to find some indication of how she should interact with Basir so she could get to know him without making him uncomfortable. She had a feeling Ryan was working with him to help him understand American ways, but she longed to understand Afghan culture. Outside of the rules for interaction between sexes, she wanted to know why Basir seemed so surprised and impressed with the meals she prepared. After learning he preferred to avoid pork and alcohol due to his upbringing in a strict Muslim home, she had set about making meals with a variety of options so she could learn what he liked and didn't like through observation. She still had no clue about his preferences, but she had learned that he would eat almost anything she offered.

The sound of approaching male voices reached her over the quiet whir of her spinning wheel. She paused in her work and glanced at the door as her brother and his friend stepped into the workshop.

"How's the barn?" she asked, since that was where she'd last seen them.

"Cleaner than it was." Ryan dropped onto his usual spot on the bench, and Basir sat beside him. "We're getting ready to head into town for a little while. Do you need anything?"

"Nothing comes to mind right off hand." She started spinning yarn again. "Will you guys be here for dinner?"

"I don't know yet. We'll have to see how it goes."

Meghan stopped the spinning wheel and lifted her head. Her brother's guarded tone reminded her way too much of when he'd first moved in with her. Ryan met her gaze, but the slight shift of his eyes toward Basir spoke louder than any words he might have said. She studied his friend and noted the same fidgetiness she'd seen in Ryan so many times at the beginning of his stay.

She smiled and nodded, certain her brother would realize she understood that where they ate depended on how Basir was handling everything. "Well, if you decide to grab something to eat while you're out, give me a call so I know not to fix dinner for you."

"No problem, sis." Ryan stood and Basir rose with him. "We'll be back later."

"Have fun."

They left the room, and Meghan looked at her spinning wheel. Making yarn was far from appealing at the moment. She couldn't get Basir out of her mind. Despite his close friendship with Ryan and the way he threw himself into helping out around the farm, he still seemed lost, as though his only goal in life was to endure whatever came his way.

"Father God," she whispered, "please help him to find his way. Guide him to the path You have chosen for him." The memory of Basir's fidgetiness intruded, and her eyes stung. "Lord, please heal him and bring him peace. I want so much to help him and comfort him the way I did Ryan when he first moved in, but I don't know how. Please guide me in my interactions with Basir, and please help him to see my words and actions in the spirit I offer them."

Although setting it all in God's hands soothed her a little, she still felt too restless to work on spinning. She left her workshop and headed outside in search of productive physical labor that might distract her.

~*~

Basir walked beside Ryan, uncomfortably aware of the looks his presence drew. Ranging from mild curiosity to almost hostile suspicion, each stare burned into him and made him wonder if moving in with Ryan and his sister had been a mistake.

"Does your town not see many strangers?" he asked after a pair of old women gaped at him then hurried away whispering.

"People pass through all the time." Ryan glanced at him and shrugged. "But I think you're the first Afghan who's ever been here."

"Hmm." Basir scanned the street, looking past the people to the town itself.

The paved street looked like so many others he had seen in America, clean and lined by sidewalks. So unlike the streets where he came from. The dust there, as well as the country's poverty, left everything looking tired and worn. Decades of war and violence had left scars everywhere, something conspicuously absent in the American cities and towns he had seen so far. Streets like the one he and Ryan currently walked along were much more common—small shops with plate glass windows, trees shading the sidewalks, planters of flowers, and an overall cared-for appearance, as though the people had reason to hope for a bright future.

Sunlight reflected off the windshield of a car parked at the curb and burned into Basir's retinas despite the dark glasses and baseball cap he wore. He stopped and closed his eyes, hoping to alleviate the pain. It lessened only slightly. Opening his eyes, he glanced at the shop beside him. It looked like some kind of café, but more importantly, it would offer a reprieve from the bright afternoon light.

He put a hand on Ryan's shoulder. "Let's go in here. My eyes have had enough sun for the moment."

"Sure. I could use something to drink anyway."

Moments later they sat in a booth on one side of the small restaurant, glasses of lemonade in front of them. Basir removed his hat but left his sunglasses on, thankful for the darkness they provided. Although he was sufficiently healed to be out of the hospital, he still had to deal with the lingering effects of his injuries. One of those effects was the light sensitivity that could trigger a migraine if he wasn't careful.

Ryan took a sip of his lemonade and studied him. "How are you doing?"

"Better." The tension in his forehead bothered him more than his eyes at the moment, but even that wasn't too bad. He could only pray it wasn't the precursor to a worse headache. Taking a sip of the sweet lemonade, he glanced at the woman peering out of the kitchen. She ducked back, the door swinging shut behind her. Basir sighed and focused on Ryan. "I think the people here are scared of me."

"I think they're more cautious than scared. They've never seen you before, but you're obviously a friend of mine. Give them time to get used to you."

Basir nodded, certain his friend was right. But he couldn't shake the feeling that they were judging him based on his ethnicity and assumed he was either a member of the Taliban or a terrorist. He had been confronted by both assumptions since coming to the United States. Although neither was correct, he couldn't stop the anger and sadness that what some of his fellow Afghans had chosen to do brought shame to them all.

"What is she doing here?" Ryan's puzzled voice broke into his thoughts.

"Who?"

"Meghan. She just parked across the street."

Basir turned to look out the windows at the front of the café, and sure enough, Meghan was climbing out of the pickup truck he'd last seen in her driveway. Clad in the same faded jeans and loose-fitting T-shirt she'd been wearing earlier, she was beautiful and modest—and undeniably American. The women in his family would never wear pants or short sleeves, especially not in public. Of course, they would never be seen in public unescorted, either.

Basir turned back to Ryan, filled with conflicting emotions and painful memories. "Don't you worry that your sister is here alone?"

"No. She was going places alone long before I moved in with her, and she'll keep doing it long after I move out." Ryan shrugged and looked past Basir again. "I know it's not what you're used to yet, but women and girls are treated equally to men in the United States. That means chaperones aren't required, they can spend time with males if they want to, and they can make their own decisions about life, marriage, and anything else."

"I understand that, but even American men must want to protect the reputations of the women in their families."

"Most of us do, yes. And if anyone spoke badly about Meghan or tried to harm her in any way, I would defend her with my life if necessary." Ryan finished his drink and set the glass aside. "It looks like she has some boxes to carry. Shall we go offer our assistance?"

"Yes. Of course." Basir gulped down the last of his lemonade and stood. As he followed Ryan through the café, he replayed their conversation in his mind. Thinking about his words now, he realized they could have been misconstrued to be an insult. When they stepped outside, Basir grabbed Ryan's hand. "Ryan, my friend, forgive me if you were offended by my questions about Meghan and protecting a woman's reputation. I meant nothing against you. I am only trying to learn."

Ryan smiled and patted him on the shoulder. "There's nothing to forgive. I know you're just trying to adjust to a culture vastly different from your own."

Before Basir could reply, an older gentleman walking toward them glared.

"Disgusting," he said as he passed and shook his head.

Basir stared after him for a moment and then looked at Ryan. "Was that comment meant for one of us?"

"I think it was meant for both of us." Ryan pulled his hand from Basir's, clearly uncomfortable. "I'm afraid that gentleman now has the wrong idea about what kind of relationship you and I have."

"Oh?"

"Two men holding hands in Afghanistan is a sign

of friendship. Two men holding hands in the United States is generally considered a sign of homosexuality."

Basir's lungs seized, making it difficult to speak. "But we are friends, nothing more."

"I know. It's just another example of the differences in our native cultures." Ryan turned toward the street. "Don't worry about it. Let's go see if Meghan wants our help."

They crossed the street, and Basir struggled to overcome the sense of shame dogging him. He hadn't meant to cause Ryan any distress by his show of friendship, but thinking back to his time working with the American military, he realized his mistake.

The soldiers and marines he'd worked with had been extremely uncomfortable with the common practices of hand holding and walking arm in arm with friends. Ryan had started out uncomfortable, but all the time he and Basir had spent together appeared to cure it. Now in the United States, however, it appeared Basir would have to be more careful about how he showed friendship to avoid causing others to get the wrong idea about the man he counted as close as a brother. He wasn't as concerned with his own reputation. His honor had already been ruined before he ever left his homeland, and he wasn't sure it could be redeemed. He planned to do his best to salvage his honor and reputation, however. To do anything less was unacceptable.

"Hey, Megs," Ryan said as they joined her at the back of the truck. "What are you doing here?"

"Julia called and asked me to bring her a load of yarn." Meghan handed her brother a cardboard box. "Since you're here, you might as well help me carry it inside."

"We were going to volunteer our services." Ryan adjusted his hold on the box and turned to Basir. "Remember that yarn Meghan was making when we left? She sells it at the little craft store down the street."

"And online, thanks to the website you helped me build." Meghan pulled another box from her truck. "That reminds me, I need your help updating the site sometime next week. I have some new photos to add and some descriptions to revise."

"Just let me know when you want to work on it."

Basir approached, uncomfortable with what he was about to do, yet knowing it was an expected part of American society. He took a deep breath and reached for the box Meghan held, reminding himself that initiating conversation with her wouldn't kill him. Ryan wouldn't kill him for it, either. "Let me carry that for you."

"Thanks, Basir." Her smile lit up the afternoon and lifted his heart as she relinquished the box.

It was lighter than he'd expected given its size. He stepped onto the sidewalk beside Ryan as Meghan pulled one more box from the truck.

"Sheesh, Megs," Ryan said as they headed down the sidewalk. "How much yarn do you think Julia needs?"

"She asked for every bit of what we're carrying. According to her, people have been coming in from nearby towns to check out the locally produced alpaca yarn." Meghan grinned, her eyes shining. "She said she can't keep it on the shelf."

"That's awesome! Congratulations!" Ryan glanced at Basir, almost as excited as his sister. "Meghan's going to be famous before long."

"Well," she said before Basir could speak, "my yarn will be famous, anyway. Of course, if sales keep rising, I'm going to need more help. Taking care of the alpacas, shearing them, prepping the wool, spinning it into yarn and packaging it, plus taking care of everything else around the farm that needs to be done already takes up most of my time. If I need to increase production, I'll have to find someone to take over some of my responsibilities."

"That's a good problem to have," Ryan said.

"Maybe, but where am I going to find someone to hire around here? This town is the size of a peanut, and everyone I know who knows anything about farming and livestock is already busy with their own operations."

Before he could consider the consequences, Basir spoke. "I could help you with the farm. I come from a rural area and know much about coaxing the land into providing for us. If you wanted, I could help more with the alpacas as well. I have sheared many sheep in my life, and alpaca wool doesn't seem to be that different."

"I've never sheared a sheep before, but collecting the alpaca wool isn't that difficult once you get the hang of it." Meghan paused outside the door to a shop and studied him. Her gaze, although much more direct than he was comfortable with from a woman, warmed him all the way thorough. And when she smiled...

Father God, help me keep my thoughts pure.

"If you want to give it a try," Meghan said, "I'd be glad to have your help. We don't need to worry about wool until spring, but there's still plenty of other work to do."

"Then I will work on your farm doing whatever

you need me to do."

"And now your problem is solved, Megs." Ryan shifted the box to one arm and opened the door, setting a strip of bells jingling merrily.

Meghan smiled as she passed through. "Thanks."

Basir followed her inside, scanning the store's interior. Fabric, yarn, thread, and many more items he couldn't identify filled the space. The products had been neatly arranged in attractive displays and aisles that invited shoppers to wander through them. An older woman with graying brown hair looked over from where she spoke with a white-haired woman by a wall lined with shelves of brightly colored fabric.

"Hi, Meghan!" she called with a friendly smile. "Just take everything to the back counter, and I'll meet you there."

"Will do." Meghan led the way around a display of plastic boxes and down an aisle of beads to a glass display case by the back wall of the shop.

Meghan set her box on the glass surface as the woman who had spoken arrived and wrapped her in a hug.

"You are a lifesaver," the woman said as she stepped back. "A knitting group is planning to be here later, and if it's anything like last time, they'll try to buy me out of yarn."

Meghan laughed and took the box her brother carried. "Well, if you need more, let me know."

"I love having a local supplier." The woman turned to Ryan with a warm smile. "Hi, Ryan. How are you?"

"I'm doing well."

"I'm glad to hear it." She shifted her gaze to Basir, who hung back feeling out of place. "Hello, there.

You're a new face to me. I'm Julia Day, the owner of this little shop."

"Hello. I am Basir Hamidi." He glanced at Ryan and wished he wasn't so uncomfortable with such outgoing behavior from women.

Ryan took the box from his hands and set it with the other two as Meghan spoke. "He worked with Ryan in Afghanistan."

Basir removed his sunglasses and hat and endured the scrutiny of the woman who apparently knew Ryan and his sister well.

"Pleased to meet you," Julia said with a friendly smile. "So, are you just visiting or have you moved to our lovely town?"

"I live here for now." In a way, he wished he could give a more definite answer on his plans, but sharing that much about his private life with a stranger didn't sit well with him. He wasn't even sure how he felt about Meghan telling her he had worked with the Americans in his homeland.

"He's going to be helping me with the farm, so I'll have more time to make yarn for you," Meghan said with a laugh.

"Wonderful!" Julia studied her, curiosity shining in her face. "Does this mean you're finally going to expand your alpaca herd like you've talked about?"

"Maybe. I'm definitely going to give it some serious consideration, anyway."

"If your yarn keeps gaining popularity, you're going to have to do it just so you'll have enough wool to keep up with the demand." Julia laughed and patted one of the boxes. "Now, let's see what you brought, and I'll write you a check."

Meghan pulled a folded piece of paper from her

back pocket. "I printed up an invoice to make it easier."

"Bless you, child," Julia said as she accepted the paper and unfolded it. "I love it when people make my job easier."

Basir was impressed with the casual yet professional way the two women handled business. It drove home the point that Meghan was indeed self-sufficient and independent. Although he wasn't used to seeing women conduct business deals, the fact that she did so with ease made him admire her.

Ryan's hand landed on his shoulder, bringing him from his thoughts.

"Since we've completed our task as delivery boys," Ryan said, "let's get out of here and leave the ladies to their work."

Basir nodded and looked away as Meghan turned toward them.

"Have you guys decided yet whether you'll be home for supper?"

Basir glanced at Ryan, leaving the decision up to him. Ryan briefly met his gaze and then looked at his sister.

"Yeah, we'll be there."

"All right. I'll see you back at the farm." She returned her attention to Julia, who was opening one of the boxes.

Basir followed Ryan to the front of the store, pulling on his hat and sunglasses before stepping outside. As they headed down the sidewalk, Basir glanced through the shop window for one last glimpse of Meghan. The question that had popped up several times since he met her rushed to the front of his mind once more.

Why wasn't such a kind, talented, and beautiful woman married?

~*~

"He's handsome," Julia said as soon as the door closed with a jingle.

"Who?" Meghan already had a pretty good idea, but sometimes playing dumb was the best option in a small town. It helped keep the gossip at bay.

"The new guy. Basir." Julia stopped examining the yarn. "But what happened to his face? Those scars look fairly recent."

"I'm not sure what happened. My brother just said he was injured, and now that he's done with physical therapy and everything, he needed a place to stay."

"Poor guy. I take it he doesn't have a family to go back to?"

"No." Meghan wasn't going to divulge what little she knew about Basir's lack of family. She'd probably already said too much, although she hadn't given any details. Not that she could even if she wanted to. The men living in her house seemed to enjoy keeping everything inside and being as vague as possible.

"Well, I'm glad he has you and your brother to help him get back on his feet." Julia pawed through another box of yarn and then stopped and met Meghan's gaze. "You know, I think he likes you."

Startled, it took Meghan a second to think. "Who? Basir?"

"I certainly don't mean Ryan," Julia said with a laugh. "You don't need to look so shocked by the idea."

"I just met him a few days ago."

"So?" Julia abandoned the box and laid a hand on Meghan's arm. "You're a beautiful person, Meghan. It doesn't take long for anyone to see that. I'd be surprised if a single man like your friend, Basir, wasn't attracted to you at least a little."

"Or maybe he's just trying to figure out his friend's sister. I think I'm a bit of an enigma to him."

"No, I don't think that's it. I take it you didn't notice the glances he kept stealing toward you? Trust me. Those were not the looks of a man trying to figure someone out. Those were the glances of a man who sees a pretty woman he would like to get to know better."

Meghan couldn't deny the ring of truth in her words. Hadn't she wondered off and on if Basir found her attractive? The times she'd caught him looking her way couldn't *all* be a matter of curiosity...could they?

The smug expression on Julia's face kept Meghan from admitting to her own suspicions, however. "You're not going to try to play matchmaker again, are you?"

"*Moi?*" Julia lifted a hand to her throat, her eyes wide with false innocence. "How could you ever suspect such a thing of me?"

"Um, let's see." Meghan tapped her chin, pretending to be deep in thought. "Do the names David Lowenstein, Brad Turner, and Mark Holcomb ring a bell?"

Julia laughed and lowered her hand. "Maybe one or two. But you can't fault me for wanting to see you happily married."

"No, I can't. You just need to realize that the happy marriage will come in God's timing, regardless of how many dates you arrange for me."

"Oh, I'm perfectly aware of that." Julia opened the third box of yarn and winked. "And I promise not to set you up with anyone else until I see whether it works out between you and Basir."

"There's nothing between us, Julia. We're barely even friends at this point."

"Give it time." She lifted out a skein of soft blue yarn. "I have a feeling your denials will fade soon enough."

Long after Meghan left the craft shop, Julia's words continued to echo in her mind. *Those were the glances of a man who sees a pretty woman he would like to get to know better.* Since her dear friend had noticed the looks as well, Meghan could no longer pretend they didn't mean anything. The question now was what exactly they *did* mean. Or maybe a better question was what, if anything, she should do with that knowledge.

Normally, she would seek advice from a friend, but that didn't seem like a viable option in this situation. With Basir's native culture being so different, any well-meant suggestions could easily offend him or cause him to get the wrong idea about her. If it were any other Afghan man, she would talk to her brother about it and see what he recommended. But since Ryan appeared oblivious to Basir's surreptitious glances in her direction, she was afraid to say anything for fear of harming the close friendship between the two men.

Meghan let herself in the back door of her house, thankful her brother's car was still gone. She needed more time to figure out how to handle everything before the guys came home. Praying God would give her the wisdom to see the path she should follow, she tried to let go of her worries so she could concentrate on preparing the sauce for that night's spaghetti.

3

As Meghan dressed in a pair of jeans and a T-shirt, she heard soft footsteps pass by her closed door. Judging by the direction they came from it was likely Basir, but why was he up so early? Every other morning, she had fed the alpacas before the guys appeared. She brushed her hair into a ponytail and continued pondering as she headed downstairs. Maybe Basir rose earlier on Sundays than any other day. Or perhaps he wasn't sleeping well. Ryan had kept strange hours for a few weeks when he first moved in. It was possible Basir would do the same thing. She could only pray he had an easier time adjusting than her brother. There had been many long nights listening to him wander restlessly through the house.

By the time she arrived at the back door and pulled on her barn shoes, she still hadn't seen any sign of her brother or Basir. Maybe she'd imagined the footsteps passing her room. They had been rather quiet, and she hadn't heard either door of the house. She chalked up the mysterious footsteps to her imagination and went outside.

The early morning quiet of the barn surrounded her as soon as she stepped inside. The only sounds came from the alpacas as they shuffled around their pens and waited for their breakfast. Meghan took a deep breath of the wood shaving and animal-scented air, relaxing in the familiar peaceful atmosphere. Then, she turned toward the feed room and nearly jumped out of her skin.

"Basir!" She placed a hand over her thundering heart as she took in the man standing in the doorway, a bucket in either hand. "What are you doing out here so early?"

"Feeding the alpacas." He lifted the buckets and then lowered them again as a crease formed between his eyebrows. "Do you not want me to feed them?"

Meghan let her hand fall to her side and drew in a steadying breath as her pulse slowed. "No, it's fine if you want to feed them. You just startled me. That's all. I didn't expect to see anyone until breakfast."

"I said I would help you with the alpacas." He glanced toward the buckets in his hands. "That is what I am doing."

"I know, and I appreciate the help. I just didn't know you planned on caring for them this morning." Meghan picked up on Basir's discomfort about the same time she realized this was the longest conversation they'd ever had—the longest they had ever been alone together. Remembering everything Ryan had told her about the cultural expectations Basir was working to overcome, she decided to leave him to his work so he could relax. "Well, if you're going to take care of these guys, I'll go start breakfast."

Basir nodded and shifted his weight. "Do you want me to put them in the pasture after they eat?"

"Yes, please. They enjoy the time in the fresh air, and it makes cleaning out their pens easier." Meghan laughed, hoping he would crack a smile. It didn't work.

"All right." He looked as serious as ever as he passed her on his way to the alpacas.

Meghan watched him dump the first bucket of feed into the trough surrounded by eager animals, and then she headed for the house. Since she was up so early and didn't have to care for the animals, she could make a more elaborate breakfast than scrambled eggs and toast. Possibilities floated through her mind as she opened the back door. The sound of dishes clanking ignited her curiosity. She kicked off her barn shoes and padded sock-footed into the kitchen.

Ryan set a mixing bowl on the counter and closed the cabinet before turning around. He grinned when his gaze fell on Meghan. "Oh, hey. I thought you'd be in the barn for a while longer."

"Not this morning. Basir volunteered to take care of the herd for me." She studied her brother, wondering if she'd missed something. "What are you doing?"

"Getting ready to make breakfast. Why?"

"You never cook."

"I cook occasionally."

Meghan rolled her eyes. "The two or three times you've been here during mealtimes and I haven't don't count."

Ryan laughed. "You have such a suspicious mind."

"I grew up with you, remember? I have every right to be suspicious when you do things out of the ordinary." She crossed her arms. "So, why the sudden urge to cook this morning when I haven't seen you this early on a Sunday morning since you moved in?"

"I'm trying to be nice, Megs." Ryan combed his fingers through his hair and sighed. "Basir and I have been talking a lot, and I realized how little I've done to help you out around here. You shouldn't have to do everything, and I'm going to make sure you don't have to as long as I'm here."

"So you're going to take over cooking?" Skepticism filled her. This was the man who had spent eight years in the Marine Corps, living in barracks, eating whatever slop they served in the mess hall or he could buy at a restaurant. Admittedly, he had picked up a few culinary skills over the years, but she doubted he knew how to cook more than a handful of dishes.

"I don't plan to cook *all* the time, but I can take care of a meal here and there just so you can have some time to relax." He stepped close and laid his hands on her shoulders. "You work hard. Too hard sometimes, especially with me and now Basir living here. I think you get so busy taking care of us, the alpacas, and your business that you forget to take care of yourself. Basir and I are going to make sure you have time for yourself. You deserve it."

The sincerity in his eyes brought tears to hers, and she wrapped her arms around him. "How did I get such a great brother?"

"Blame it on Mom and Dad. They raised me."

"I think I can also thank the marines." She stepped back and smiled. "They helped you become an even better man, Ryan."

"They taught me what's really important in life, anyway." He glanced toward the bowl he had set on the counter and then returned his gaze to her. "So, are you going to let me fix breakfast this morning?"

Meghan debated for a moment, but then she saw how much it meant to him. "Sure. Go ahead."

"Thanks, Megs." Her brother's smile was worth feeling a little lost with no responsibilities for the first time in years. "Now, get out of here and go take a bubble bath or something."

"A bubble bath?" She laughed and shook her head.

"Isn't that what all women do to relax?"

"I have no clue, but this woman would prefer a long, hot shower instead of having to rush to get ready for church." Meghan headed for the hall, her heart lightened by the generosity of the men living in her house. "See you at breakfast!"

~*~

Basir couldn't keep his eyes off Meghan during breakfast. He gave it his best attempt, but no matter how determined he was not to stare, his gaze was inevitably drawn to her over and over. In the time it had taken him to care for the animals and Ryan to cook breakfast, she had transformed herself from the casual farming woman into a beauty like no other. Her brown hair shone, and she had created two small braids that ran from her temples to the back of her head where they merged into one. The rest of her hair hung loose, flowing in a rich curtain down her back. A light amount of makeup enhanced her eyes and made her lips shimmer. And her dress...

He looked away again, but the vision was burned into his brain. The soft-looking green fabric of her dress matched her eyes, and the cut highlighted her amazing figure while still keeping her covered and modest. If this was the result of her having extra time to herself, he wasn't sure how he was going to keep his attraction to her hidden for long. Instead of waiting until he had rebuilt his reputation and redeemed his honor to the extent he could, he might have to admit to his feelings for his best friend's sister much sooner. Surely, Ryan would notice his inability to avoid looking at Meghan. Better to be honest than have him worry Basir had improper intentions toward her.

Yet throughout the meal, Ryan seemed oblivious. He chatted with both Basir and Meghan, appearing as though he hadn't a care in the world. Hope rose in Basir's chest as he helped Ryan clear the table while Meghan left the room. Maybe he wouldn't have to speak up before he was ready after all.

"I should have talked to you a long time ago," Ryan said as he stacked dishes in the dishwasher.

Basir's blood froze. "Oh?"

"Yeah. Meghan's more relaxed this morning than I've seen her in a long time." Ryan smiled and closed the dishwasher. "If I'd talked to you sooner, maybe I could have kept her from being under such a strain for so long."

"Would she have listened before now?" Basir drew in a slow breath and released it just as slowly. Ryan wasn't going to take him to task for looking at Meghan after all.

"Probably not. She's as stubborn as me...maybe more so," Ryan said with a laugh.

"But that stubbornness has served you well." He remembered a few times when Ryan's persistence had done much to help the American cause. "Perhaps it serves her just as well."

"Oh, I know for a fact it does. Take a look at this farm and her yarn business. Our parents thought she was nuts for buying this place and going into business for herself. Our dad was sure she would fail in the first year. Our mom figured she would make it two years before having to give it up. But Meghan refused to

36

listen to their dire predictions and similar ones from others, and now six years later her business is still growing."

"She has done well for herself."

"Yeah, she has. I'm proud of her accomplishments. Now if I could manage to find a job or some kind of career that I love as much as she loves the life she's built, maybe someone could be proud of my accomplishments."

Although his words could have indicated jealousy, Basir heard only sadness in his friend's voice. He walked over and put a hand on Ryan's shoulder, looking him in the eye. "Many people are proud of your accomplishments already. Didn't you receive commendations from your commander? Didn't your family write to tell you they were proud of you? And didn't you gain the respect of the village elders when it mattered most?"

"Yes, but that was all during my time in the marines. I'm a civilian now, and I've accomplished nothing other than moving in with my sister because I have no job and no home of my own." Ryan sighed and shook his head. "Meghan has assured me I can stay here as long as I need to, but I'm starting to feel like I'm a burden to her."

"I don't think she sees you as a burden. You are her brother, and she cares for you."

"That's the problem. She shouldn't have to take care of me. I'm a marine, for Pete's sake." Ryan groaned and thrust his fingers into his hair. "I need to find a way to be independent again."

Basir understood the sentiment completely. Having to rely on Ryan and Meghan for care was difficult, but he appreciated their generosity toward a man who had nothing. "Perhaps it is time you sought employment."

"I think it is." Ryan inhaled deeply then blew out the breath. "For today, I need to relax. I can start looking for work tomorrow. Just don't tell Meghan that's what I'm planning to do. I don't want to get her hopes up and then not be able to find a job."

"I will not say a word."

"I knew I could count on you."

They left the kitchen and Meghan met them in the hallway, a purse over her shoulder and a Bible in her hand. "Hey, I almost forgot I have to get to the church early this morning to help set up. If you guys are ready to go, you're welcome to ride with me."

"You go ahead," Ryan said. "I'll drive us over in a little while."

"All right. I'll see you there." She went out the front door.

Basir wished he could have gone with her, but he didn't dare unless he wanted Ryan questioning him about his interest in her. He wasn't ready for that conversation so close to moving in with them. There were still too many things he needed to work through first, too many ways he wasn't good enough for Meghan. Perhaps someday that would change, but for now he needed to focus on anything but possibly having a relationship with her.

He rubbed his forehead to relieve the building tension, and Ryan gave him a concerned look.

"You OK?"

The pressure eased slightly, and Basir nodded as he lowered his hand. "For now."

"Do you need to stay home and rest? It's OK if you do."

Although his doctors would probably recommend it, he couldn't do it. He needed to go to church today. Faith had always been a mainstay in his life, and he needed the time in worship to get through the coming week.

"No, I will be OK. I have medicine I can take with me in case a migraine develops."

"Well, if you need to leave early, just let me know."

"I will." Basir headed upstairs, praying his headache wouldn't get any worse before it went away.

Only a vague ache remained in his skull when they arrived at the small church. Hope rose that perhaps he could avoid worse pain, and he followed Ryan inside. The warm greetings of the congregants lifted Basir's heart and affirmed he had made the right decision by coming. This fellowship with other believers was what he needed after the turmoil of losing one temporary home and moving into another with a beautiful woman he couldn't keep out of his thoughts.

Throughout Sunday school, Basir struggled to concentrate on the lesson. Between Meghan sitting across the room from him and the headache flaring to life, his distraction levels were at an all-time high. The concerned glances Ryan kept giving him didn't help matters any. By the time the class ended, Basir knew he should have stayed home. Unfortunately, that knowledge did nothing to help him now.

He followed Ryan to a large room with a table at one end and groups of people scattered around as they talked. The table held a coffee urn and an assortment of cookies, but neither held any appeal for Basir. All he wanted to do was go somewhere dark and quiet and hope the pain stabbing his brain would dissipate quickly.

"You want some coffee?" Ryan asked as they headed toward the table.

"No." Basir drew in a deep breath and slowly released it, knowing it was time to take his meds before his migraine got worse. "Where can I get some water?"

"In the kitchen." Ryan studied him briefly. "You look terrible."

"My head is about to explode."

"Come with me."

Basir followed him through a doorway on the far side of the room. Thankfully, the small kitchen was quieter and vacant of people. He leaned against a counter and closed his eyes as Ryan dug through a cabinet. From the rapidly worsening symptoms, Basir had a feeling the medicine wouldn't help enough. It might alleviate a little of the pain, but he doubted it would enable him to survive the worship service.

Footsteps approached, and he opened his eyes, squinting as the light hit his already sensitive eyes. Ryan handed him a foam cup filled with water.

"Thank you." Basir pulled the prescription bottle from his pocket. After taking a dose, he shoved the bottle back in his pocket and set the water on the counter. "I hate to say it, but I think I should go home."

"That's fine." Ryan gripped his shoulder and gave him a sympathetic smile. "I'll go find Meghan and let her know we're leaving, then I'll come back and get you."

"All right." Basir closed his eyes again and hoped the medicine would take effect soon.

4

Meghan watched Ryan come out of the kitchen and stop to talk to the pastor. She didn't see Basir anywhere, however, and that concerned her. He hadn't looked good during Sunday school. His swarthy skin had been a little pale, and the tightness in his face had left her wondering if he was in pain.

Before she could ponder his absence any further, Ryan joined her. "Hey, can you run Basir back to the house? A migraine has decided to attack him, and Pastor Joel just reminded me that I'm helping with junior church this morning."

"Of course I'll give him a ride, but will he go with me?"

"With as miserable as he is right now, I think he will." Ryan sighed and combed his fingers through his hair. "I really hate putting either one of you in an uncomfortable position, but I'm obligated to stay."

Meghan smiled and patted his arm. "Don't worry about it. We'll both be fine, and maybe this will help him see that it's OK to talk to me without a chaperone hanging around."

"Maybe." Ryan released a breath. "Let's go tell him you're driving him instead of me."

She followed her brother toward the kitchen, prayers for Basir and the coming drive flowing from her heart in a continuous stream. With as reserved as he'd been around her since the moment they met, she had a feeling being alone with her for an extended period was going to be hard on him. Since he was already suffering, she could only hope that his discomfort around her wouldn't make it worse.

As soon as they stepped into the kitchen, she spotted Basir sitting on a stool with his head in his hands as he massaged his scalp. From his strained expression, the motion of his fingers wasn't helping.

"Change of plans," Ryan said as he approached his friend. "I forgot I'm helping with the kids this morning, so Meghan's going to give you a ride."

Basir lifted his head, his eyes wide. "Ryan..."

"It'll be fine. She's just going to take you back to the house, and then she'll leave you alone. I'll be there as soon as the service ends."

Meghan watched his struggle and tried not to feel hurt by his obvious reluctance to go with her. It was a cultural thing, not a personal one. The memory of all his surreptitious glances and Julia's comments about him liking her were enough to help her remember that. If only he could get past whatever held him back from pursuing any kind of relationship with her, she would agree to a conversation, a date, or whatever he wanted to do so they could get to know each other.

For now, however, they had to convince him to get in her truck.

Ryan leaned close to him and said something Meghan couldn't make out. After a moment, Basir sighed and nodded. Ryan clapped a hand to his shoulder and smiled as he turned to Meghan.

"I'll see you guys as soon as I can get out of here." He left the kitchen.

She took a hesitant step toward Basir, unsure of how he would react to her approaching. "Are you ready to go?"

"Yes." He slid off the stool and grimaced. His eyes closed briefly, and then he looked in her general direction without actually looking at her. He placed his hand over his heart. "I appreciate you giving me a ride. Thank you."

"I'm glad to do it."

He bowed his head and then straightened and moved to the door. Meghan walked with him through the church and out to the parking lot. As soon as he sat in the passenger seat, he leaned his head back and closed his eyes. Meghan started the engine and drove toward the farm, thankful her brother had been right, but she was also worried. How miserable must Basir be for him to agree so easily to go somewhere alone with a single woman?

By the time she parked in her usual spot near the back of the house, she'd decided that his headache had to be horrible to make him willing to be alone and unchaperoned with her. Although he hadn't said anything, his grimaces and occasional soft groans had let her know how much he suffered.

She shut off the engine and pulled the keys from the ignition. When Basir didn't move, she spoke quietly. "We're here."

He gave a slight nod and opened his door. Meghan climbed out and let them in the back door of the house. She followed him to the stairs, unsure if he could make it to his room on his own. He seemed a little unsteady. When he started up the stairs, he paused on the third step and grabbed the handrail as he swayed. Worry slammed into her, and she hurried to his side.

"Are you OK?"

"A little dizzy." He closed his eyes and sighed.

Meghan didn't want to risk him falling down the steps, so she slipped an arm around his waist. His eyes popped open, and he stared at her.

"Meghan..." His voice sounded unnaturally tight.

She lifted his arm and placed it over her shoulders. "I'm just making sure you get to your room without falling. If it helps, think of me as a nurse."

"But you are Ryan's sister."

"And you think nurses don't have brothers?" She shook her head and put her foot on the next step. "Let's go."

They slowly climbed the stairs, and by the time they reached Basir's room, he was leaning on Meghan for support. She helped him to his bed and eased him onto the mattress. He stretched out with a groan and closed his eyes. Still acting as a nurse, Meghan moved to the foot of the bed, removed his shoes, and set them on the floor. Then she returned to his side and lifted his glasses from his face. As she laid them on the nightstand, Basir opened his eyes and looked up at her.

She offered a smile. "I'll go get a cool cloth to place over your eyes. That's helped me through some awful headaches."

She left the room before he could speak and went into the bathroom. Moments later, she returned with a damp, folded washcloth. Basir had closed his eyes again, and a grimace marred his handsome face. Sympathy flooded through her at the sight of his pain, and she moved to his side.

"Keep your eyes closed," she said softly. "I'm going to put a damp cloth over them."

He did as instructed, and she laid the washcloth in place. Unable to resist, she gently smoothed the thick dark hair away from his forehead.

"Thank you." His quiet voice startled her. "Compassion shines brighter through you than Kashmala."

Certain it was a compliment but unsure of its meaning, she didn't know how to reply. Finally, she settled on patting his shoulder. "I'll get out of here and let you rest. If you need anything, just holler."

She left the room, closing the door about halfway, and went downstairs.

When her brother arrived home, Meghan was in the kitchen making brownies.

"Hey," Ryan said as he entered the room. "How's Basir?"

"Sleeping, I hope." She slid the pan into the oven then faced him. "What's Kashmala?"

"What?" His eyes widened. "Where did you hear that name?"

"From Basir." She peered at him, wondering why he appeared so startled by a simple word. "So, Kashmala is a who, not a what?"

"She was a who, anyway." He pulled out a chair at the table and dropped into it.

Meghan joined him, more curious than ever about Basir's compliment. "Who was she?"

Ryan stared at the tabletop for several seconds before finally speaking. "Kashmala was his wife. She was killed a few years ago."

"Poor Basir." Tears stung Meghan's eyes at the thought of such a young man losing his wife.

"He told me when he found out, but that's the only time he's ever mentioned her to me. I didn't even know he had a wife before that day." Ryan met Meghan's gaze. "Why did he mention her to you?"

"I don't know." Now that she knew who Kashmala was, Meghan was more confused than ever. "He said something about compassion shining brighter through me than her."

"You've really made an impression on him." Ryan combed his fingers through his short hair. "I should warn you that saying anything to him about Kashmala, even just a sympathetic comment about her death, is probably a bad idea unless he mentions her first. Afghan men tend to be very private when it comes to the women in their families."

"Is that why you looked so shocked when I asked about her name?"

"Yeah. It's a name I never thought I'd hear again." Ryan stood and pushed his chair under the table. "I should go check on Basir, see if he needs anything."

Meghan watched him leave the room, her mind racing. Why had Basir mentioned the name of his dead wife to a woman he had known only a few days? From what Ryan said, he never talked about her even to people he knew well. Then again, why imply that Meghan was more compassionate than the woman he had married?

The more she learned about Basir, the less she understood and the more curious she became.

~*~

A familiar double tap on the door sank into Basir's subconscious, and he opened his eyes to find a blurry version of Ryan standing in the doorway.

"Hey," Ryan said quietly and stepped closer to the bed. "How are you doing?"

"Better, but still not good." Basir sighed and rolled

onto his back. "How was church?"

"The part I was in the sanctuary for was good. Then, I was in a classroom with about fifteen kids who were determined to see how crazy they could make us during their lesson and craft."

"You sound like you enjoyed it anyway." Basir reached for his glasses—trying to focus on a blurry world threatened to make his migraine worse again.

"I did. Those kids may be a handful, but I love working with them." Ryan sat down on the foot of the bed and studied him. "How did it go with Meghan bringing you home?"

"Your sister is very kind. She told me to think of her as a nurse when she helped me come up here." He looked at Ryan, hoping his friend wouldn't be angry that she had touched him again. "The headache made me dizzy, and she was afraid I would fall without her supporting me."

"She's great about helping people when they need it." Ryan stayed quiet just long enough for Basir to worry about his next words. "She said you told her she's compassionate."

"Yes, I did." He still couldn't believe he'd mentioned his wife to her. That had been a slip he regretted instantly and hoped wouldn't come back to haunt him. When he said it, however, it had come straight from his heart. He shoved the thought aside, unable to consider the implications at the moment. "Your sister is a very compassionate woman."

"More compassionate than Kashmala?"

Hearing her name from the man who had offered consolation when Basir learned of her murder sent a jolt to his heart. He closed his eyes as memories flashed of his temperamental wife and the message he had received two days after her death. Guilt flooded him anew at the reminder he hadn't been able to protect her from the Taliban—from the men who had killed her in retaliation for him assisting the Americans.

"I'm sorry," Ryan said. "I shouldn't have said that."

Basir drew in a steadying breath and opened his eyes again. "No, you are right to question my choice of words to your sister. Meghan...she is...forgive me."

Admitting the truth was more difficult than he'd expected. Unfortunately, he had to carry through with it or risk losing the respect of a man he admired. "Your sister is more compassionate than my wife ever was. Kashmala was a beautiful woman, but I don't think she liked me very much. Our families arranged our marriage, thinking we would be a good match. We were not, but we did the best we could under the circumstances."

"Did you love her?"

He should have known Ryan would ask the same question he had wondered many times since his wedding. "I loved her as much as I could, but not as much as I wanted to. She was a difficult woman and never understood my choice to become an interpreter. I did care about her and would have given my life to save hers, but I failed her."

"There was nothing you could have done, Basir. Even if you had been home with her, they would have killed her anyway and killed you as well."

Ryan had told him the same thing when Basir confided in him about her death. At the time, the words hadn't done anything to lessen the pain of knowing he had failed in his job as a husband to protect his wife. Now that he had seen and lived through so much more violence, the truth in them helped ease the lingering guilt.

Basir nodded and released a cleansing breath. "What did you tell Meghan about Kashmala?"

"Just that she was your wife and had been killed. Anything else should come from you."

"Will I need to tell her more?" He hadn't considered that one mention of Kashmala could force him to divulge more information than he was comfortable sharing with a woman he still wasn't sure he should be alone with.

"That's up to you." Ryan smiled sympathetically. "If you decide to tell her anything, you'll see more of her compassionate nature. And I can guarantee she won't hold anything you say against you. She's the most understanding and forgiving person I've ever met."

Much like her brother. Ryan had done more to help him adapt to the American culture than anyone else, and he had forgiven every faux pas Basir committed. Since picking him up and bringing him to the farm, Ryan had continued to prove his understanding and forgiving nature was still alive and well.

With that thought in mind, Basir realized he had nothing to fear when it came to his attraction to Meghan. If Ryan approved, there would be no problem. If he didn't, he would undoubtedly forgive Basir's interest. The situation was a delicate one, however, and called for caution.

"Your sister would make a good friend."

"She'd like it if you became her friend. As it stands now, she's not sure if you like her or trust her since you rarely talk to her and are obviously uncomfortable being alone with her."

"I only wish to give her the respect she deserves as your sister and a woman." Hope rose in Basir. Perhaps the attraction wasn't one-sided.

"I know, but you have to keep in mind that respect here and respect where you're from don't always look the same. If you want to be her friend, talk to her. Get to know her. As long as you don't mistreat her, I'm sure your respect for her will still show through."

Basir kept his breathing even as his heart thundered with excitement. It sounded as though Ryan approved of him for Meghan. There was just one more thing he needed to know. "Forgive me if you are offended, but why is your sister not married? In my culture, she would have been married years ago."

"She hasn't met the right man yet. Remember Julia, the woman at the craft store? She keeps trying to help Meghan find someone to marry by setting her up with any eligible man she comes across. Meghan usually goes on one date with each guy as a courtesy, but she has yet to meet the man God has chosen for her."

Dating was something Basir still wasn't sure he understood. He'd heard about it from the Americans while he was still in Afghanistan. Since coming to the United States, he had heard about the various dating lives of nurses and physical therapists. While the process sounded interesting if frustrating, he had never been on a date in his life. It wasn't permitted where he came from.

Thinking about the implied consent of Ryan, Basir wasn't sure yet what to do about developing a relationship with Meghan. There were still so many reasons he wasn't a good option for her, not the least of which being that he had brought shame upon himself and his family by working with the Americans and not protecting his wife. But he was drawn to Meghan and wanted to follow Ryan's advice by getting to know her.

The dilemma renewed the pounding in his head. He sighed and closed his eyes. The bed shifted, and Basir opened his eyes to find Ryan standing.

"I should get out of here and let you rest." He moved the door and then looked back. "Do you need anything before I go?"

"An instant cure for migraines?"

Ryan chuckled and shook his head. "Wish I could give you one, but I don't think such a thing exists."

"It doesn't. I don't need anything except for this headache to go away."

"Well, I'll pray it will leave you soon. If you need anything before then, Meghan and I will both be around."

"Thank you." Basir closed his eyes as he listened to Ryan step into the hallway. The migraines and the light sensitivity in his eyes were two more reasons he wasn't a good match for Meghan. At least the sunglasses a marine had insisted he try on just before the blast had prevented total blindness. Still, what woman as independent as Meghan would want a man who had such serious physical weaknesses? Yet Basir couldn't shake the sense that she wouldn't care if he wore dark glasses for the rest of his life and had daily headaches severe enough to make him wish his head would explode—just to get it over with.

Was it his own longing for companionship that attracted him to Meghan despite all the reasons it wasn't a good idea, or was it God leading him to her?

~*~

Meghan stirred the pot on the stove one more time and took a deep breath of the rich, chicken-scented steam. Although she hadn't originally planned to make chicken vegetable soup for lunch, she'd changed the menu in deference to Basir's misery. She had no idea if he would want to eat anything, but soup seemed like the best option in case he did.

Ryan walked into the kitchen as she turned the burner down to a simmer. "How's lunch?"

"Ready whenever we are." She turned around, her thoughts drifting to the man upstairs. "Should I let Basir know there's soup if he wants it?"

Her brother scrubbed a hand across the back of his neck. "You might wait a little while. Talking to me seemed to wear him out, and he looked like he was about to take a nap when I left."

"OK."

Meghan moved to the cabinet to retrieve two bowls. She still wondered about that conversation. Ryan had come downstairs and gone straight outside without a word. When he returned fifteen minutes later, he claimed he had just gone out to check the alpacas, but she had a feeling it was more than that. He'd had the same distant look she had seen way too many times since he moved in—the look that meant he was remembering something he would rather forget.

She ladled the soup into the bowls, and Ryan carried them to the table. Once they were eating, she decided the best approach was straightforward. "How did the conversation with Basir go?"

"Fine, I guess." Ryan ate a bite of his lunch and then set his spoon in the bowl with a sigh. "He's had a rough life, Megs. I know you think I had a lot of problems when I moved in, but I think he's got more."

Worry stabbed her heart. "Does he need to see a therapist?"

"I don't know, but that's not why I'm bringing it up." Ryan drew in a deep breath and slowly released it. "He seems interested in becoming your friend, but he's not sure how to do it."

"That's easy. All he has to do is talk to me and quit looking like he wishes the ground would swallow him when he's in the same room with me and you're not."

"It's not that simple for him. He's trying to adjust to American society, and he's done a great job of it so far. But it's like moving here has set back his attempts to leave Afghan culture behind. It doesn't help that the confidence and strength he had when I knew him in Afghanistan seem to have vanished in the explosion that brought him here." He leaned forward and looked her straight in the eye. "He's afraid he's going to accidentally disrespect you by doing something we find perfectly normal but is completely foreign to him."

"Poor guy." How she wished she could wave a magic wand and heal whatever hurts and fears rested inside him.

"Yeah, but that's one of the reasons I said he has problems. He's got a lot to work through and deal with, but he does want to be your friend."

"What should I do to help him realize it's OK to talk to me?" Another thought struck. "Is there anything I can do?"

"Keep being friendly. Try to talk to him more." Ryan relaxed against the back of his chair. "I know you've been holding back, trying to help him feel more comfortable, but I don't think it's doing him any favors. Just be yourself. He's going to be uncomfortable for a while, but I think it'll be good for him in the long run to see what normal American interaction between men and women looks like."

"I'll do what I can." Meghan scooped up a carrot chunk. "But I'll warn you now that if being myself is too hard on him, I'm backing off again until he's ready for more."

"That's fine. I want to see him become as American as we are, but I doubt that will ever fully happen. He's got too much Afghan life ingrained in him."

"That's what happens when you're born in Afghanistan and live there for most of your life." Meghan smiled and watched her brother take another bite. "Don't worry. We'll figure out this friendship thing, and I seriously doubt it will kill either one of us."

Ryan chuckled and shook his head. "It may not kill you, but life around here is probably going to be awkward for a while until he adjusts to his new country's ways."

As they continued their meal, Meghan said a silent prayer for Basir. She had a feeling he would need all the Divine assistance he could get in the coming days, but she knew her brother was right. Basir would eventually adjust to life in the United States, and the best way she could help him was to be friendly until he relaxed and realized friendship with a single woman wouldn't hurt either of them. But would it stay just a friendship?

Meghan wasn't sure her brother had noticed the budding attraction between his friend and her. For the moment, she didn't mind. Ryan had always been protective of her, and more than one potential boyfriend had wondered how long he would live if he did anything even remotely wrong. Would Ryan act the same way with Basir, a man he knew and trusted like family?

She still hadn't come up with an answer by the time they finished lunch and Ryan wandered off. After washing the few dishes they'd used, Meghan headed for the stairs. She had no idea if it had been long enough to safely disturb Basir, but she couldn't refrain any longer from seeing if he wanted anything to eat. Letting anyone go hungry wasn't in her nature, and she had that nudge in her heart that said she needed to do whatever she was considering.

Silence reigned on the second floor, and doubts assailed her as she approached Basir's room. The door stood ajar, and she gave a light knock as she peered into the room. Basir still lay on the bed, although he'd removed the cloth she had placed over his eyes. He opened them and looked toward the door before she could back away.

Uncertain of how poor his eyesight was, she smiled and opened the door a little farther as she spoke. "Hey, I just thought I'd see if you wanted anything to eat. I made some chicken vegetable soup for lunch. If that doesn't sound good, I can fix you something else."

"The soup is fine. Thank you." He sat up, swung his legs over the side of the bed, and rubbed his eyes before reaching for his glasses.

"How are you feeling?"

"Much better than when you helped me up here." He settled his glasses in place and stood.

"I'm glad to hear it." Meghan led the way downstairs, thrilled that her brother's pep talk had apparently soaked into Basir. Although a little stilted and sparse, his attempt at conversation warmed her heart.

She settled him at the kitchen table with a bowl of soup and then set about preparing a batch of icing for the brownies. While she didn't mind unfrosted brownies, her brother loved the added bit of sweetness. Basir finished off a second bowl of soup while she frosted and cut the brownies.

As he carried his bowl to the sink, she indicated the pan on the counter in front of her. "Would you like a brownie? I'm about to go tell Ryan they're ready."

Basir slowly set his dish in the sink. "I will wait until you return."

"All right. I'll be back in a minute."

She left the kitchen and followed the sounds of music and explosions to the living room. As she'd expected, Ryan had sprawled on the sofa and was playing one of the video games he'd brought with him. When she stopped just inside the doorway, he paused the game and looked up.

"Brownies are ready, and I fed Basir lunch."

"Really?" Ryan laid the controller aside and stood. "I didn't hear him come downstairs."

"He's been down here long enough to eat two bowls of soup."

"Sounds like his migraine is gone."

"So, do you want a brownie?"

"Do you really have to ask?" Ryan grinned and moved toward the hall.

Meghan laughed and followed him to the kitchen.

5

Basir followed the sound of voices to Meghan's workshop and found her and her brother huddled before a computer on the desk against the back wall. Curiosity about what held their attention propelled him into the room. Ryan looked up and grinned.

"Hey, you want to learn how to update a website? That way Meghan can bug you when she needs help with it."

All words temporarily flew from Basir's mind, and then he realized his friend was teasing. He chuckled and shook his head. "I will leave the website updating to you. The alpacas and I get along too well for me to want to take on a different job."

Meghan turned toward him, her smile warming the chill that seemed to be a permanent part of his soul lately. "Why don't you grab that stool and bring it over here? We'll let Ryan do all the hard work, but you can help me decide which pictures to use and whether the writing sounds too dorky."

Although doubtful about the wisdom of sitting so close to her, Basir went to the spinning wheel and retrieved the stool she'd indicated. He set it next to her and received smiles from both her and Ryan as he settled onto it.

"So, which photo do you like better?" Meghan indicated two images of the alpaca herd on the screen. "Ryan and I have a difference of opinion on which one is better, so you get the deciding vote."

The weight of responsibility settled on Basir's shoulders, making him uncomfortable. What did he know about good photographs for websites? Until he started working for the Americans, he had never even seen a computer.

But he couldn't resist the hopeful glimmer in Meghan's eyes. He looked at the two images, noticing subtle differences between them. Both were good, clear photographs showing the alpacas in a pasture. He could see either one working just fine on a website, but there had to be a reason Meghan and Ryan couldn't agree.

"What do you hope the photograph will do?"

"It's not so much that the photo will do anything," Meghan said, leaning back in her chair. "I just want to show where the wool for the yarn comes from. Think of it as a way to add character to the site, give it a little atmosphere."

The small bit of information helped, but he still felt he needed more to be able to make the best decision. "May I see your website?"

"Sure. Hang on just a second." Two clicks later, she had pulled up a website in pastel colors with the name "Carpenter Alpacas" in a script that looked almost like handwriting curving across the top. "I want to put the photo of the herd right here."

She tapped the screen, indicating a cartoon image of a chubby alpaca. Basir studied the clean lines of the site's appearance and the overall welcoming feel of it. He had an idea of which photo would fit better with the style, but he needed to make sure.

"May I see the photos again?"

Meghan returned them to the screen, and Basir

nodded. Only one would give the effect she wanted. He leaned forward and tapped the one on the right.

"Use this one. It fits better with your website."

"Yes!" Meghan grinned and turned to her brother. "I told you so."

Ryan studied the screen for a moment then met Basir's gaze. "I don't see whatever you guys are seeing. Why is this one better than the other one?"

"The light is softer," Basir said, torn between wishing Meghan would quit staring at him and wishing she would look at him forever. "The alpacas are more relaxed. And I like the way the fence is shown in the bottom half. It shows the alpacas are cared for, rather than being left on their own."

"Hmm." Ryan studied the screen for a moment and nodded. "Yeah, OK. I get it now. I just thought the other one was better because of the bolder look to it and the lack of fence. But now that you've explained it, the softer photo does make more sense for the site's design. Meghan's yarn is all about softness and comfort, and there's something relaxing about the photo you guys like."

Meghan's eyes widened. Then, she grinned and turned toward Basir. She reached a hand toward his arm, and he tensed, preparing for a touch he would undoubtedly love, but her brother might not approve. At the last second, she stopped and pulled her hand away before making even the slightest contact.

"I should get you to back me up against Ryan more often. He's a hardheaded pain in the rear when he makes his mind up about something, but you're good at persuading him to quit being stubborn and consider another option."

Basir was only mildly surprised at the

disrespectful way she spoke about her brother. One thing he had noticed during his time with the American military and since coming to the United States was that seemingly insulting words could actually indicate affection, depending on the speaker's tone of voice and expression. Meghan's made it clear she loved her brother.

"I only told him why I chose the photograph I did," Basir said quietly, unsure if he needed to explain. "He is the one who opened his mind in order to understand."

"Hey, I learned a long time ago to trust your judgment." Ryan leaned forward and took control of the computer's mouse. "Let me put this where Meghan wants it."

They discussed a handful of other photographs showing yarn, wool, and Meghan's workshop. Then, they turned their attention to the descriptions on the website. Basir wished he could slip away without insulting anyone, but he felt honor-bound to stay and help if he could. Although he spoke English fluently due to his time working with the Americans and thanks to a pair of university students who had lived and worked with his family for a year, his reading skills were well below the average American man. Ryan had helped him learn to read well enough to get by, but deciding whether writing on a website was any good went way beyond his abilities.

Meghan pointed to a block of text on a page labeled *About the Yarn*. "I'm just not sure this sounds good. What do you guys think? Should I update it or leave it the way it is?"

Basir looked at the screen, but the small print was difficult for him to decipher. He didn't want to admit to Meghan how poorly he read. She already knew enough about him to humiliate him. Adding another bit of ammunition to that arsenal was a bad idea.

"I think it sounds pretty good." Ryan looked at Basir, his expression as indecipherable as the words on the screen. "What do you think?"

How could his friend put him on the spot like that? Ryan knew he didn't read well. Basir shook his head and reined in his irritation. "I don't know."

"Surely you have an opinion." Meghan studied him, her gaze more intense than he liked. "You had such great input on the photos."

"I am better with pictures than words." Basir looked away and tried to find a graceful way to get out of providing an opinion on something he didn't understand. Then a thought sprang to mind, and hope filled him once more. "Why don't you read it out loud? Sometimes hearing the words instead of just reading them makes a difference."

Meghan slowly nodded and looked at the computer once more. "That makes sense."

Basir caught Ryan's approving look, but he couldn't help feeling like he was being dishonest by not admitting to his difficulty with reading. Would Meghan, with her kind nature and understanding ways, be ashamed of his ignorance? Or was he only worried because of the shame he felt at being uneducated in a well-educated world?

Meghan's voice interrupted his thoughts. "Raised on thirty acres of rolling pasture, each alpaca receives the best care to insure only the highest quality wool is produced. Regular grooming keeps the wool in top shape until the day the animals are sheared. Once the fiber has been properly washed and prepared, Meghan

Carpenter spins the wool by hand into beautiful yarn with a fine texture that creates a lovely drape in whatever fabric is made of the yarn."

The last sentence caught Basir's attention, and he pointed to it on the screen. "This sounds a little awkward. Perhaps take out some of the description?"

"Hmm..." Meghan studied the words then turned toward him. "What should I take out? I agree that it's awkward as written, but I'm not sure how to improve it."

He considered possible ways to change the description, but only one seemed to work well. "What if you change it to something like, 'Once the wool has been washed and prepared, Meghan Carpenter spins it by hand into yarn that provides a lovely drape to any fabric it is used to make'?"

"That does sound better." Meghan glanced at her brother. "What do you think?"

"I think Basir may have a hidden talent as an editor." Ryan winked and reached for the keyboard. "I'll have the change made in a jiffy."

~*~

The sun shone down with burning intensity as Meghan yanked a weed from the garden. Why was it men always complained about women taking forever? Basir had promised to help her weed the garden this morning, but he still hadn't come outside. Was he having second thoughts about working alone with her for that length of time?

After yesterday's web design session, she'd thought he was over his shyness. Well, mostly over it, anyway. He had still looked to Ryan for permission or confirmation or something quite often while they discussed the updates, but he'd carried on a conversation with her and hadn't appeared to suffer too much. Then this morning over breakfast when she mentioned needing to weed the garden, he had volunteered to help without the slightest hesitation.

Now that it was time to actually come out and help her, however, his courage seemed to have disappeared. With any luck, Ryan could give him a quick pep talk and kick him out the door. As much as she wanted the unusual man living in her house to be comfortable, right at the moment she would prefer having his assistance regardless of how uncomfortable he was. Without it, she was liable to still be weeding when the sun was at its hottest.

The back door closed with a quiet thud, and Meghan breathed a sigh of relief. Basir must have finally come to his senses and realized helping her in the garden wouldn't kill him after all. She pulled a cluster of weeds and the lack of approaching footsteps sank in.

Tossing the handful of weeds in the bucket by her bare feet, she straightened and found Basir standing on the back steps, the brim of his baseball cap pulled low and his big black sunglasses in place as he watched her. She offered him a friendly smile in the hope it would allay whatever fears or doubts were keeping him from approaching.

"Hey, Basir, if you want to start on the other side, I'll meet you in the middle."

He looked away without responding, the lean muscles in his body showing his tension. Before she could speak again, he descended the steps and headed toward the pastures.

Meghan blew out an exasperated breath and swatted a strand of hair away from her eyes. So much for the promised help. She shook her head and returned to her work, muttering, "I meant the other side of the garden, not the other side of the farm."

Why couldn't the man just relax and realize she wasn't going to hate him for being friendly? Each time she thought he might be making progress toward integrating into American society, he seemed to take a step back and resist it. Ryan's comments to her Sunday afternoon sprang to mind, and guilt pinged her heart. Maybe her brother was right and Basir did have more problems. If those problems were interfering with his ability to adapt, she couldn't hold it against him. She wasn't sure she could hold cultural reservations against him, either. But if it was something psychological that he couldn't control, she definitely needed to show more understanding and offer as much support as he would accept.

Ryan came outside as she dumped her bucket of weeds and dead leaves into the wheelbarrow at the end of the garden. He scanned the area, his expression puzzled. "Where's Basir? I thought he was going to help you weed."

"So did I." Meghan set her bucket on the ground and swiped the back of her wrist across her sweaty forehead. "He came out, stared at me for a minute, and left."

"That's weird." A furrow formed between Ryan's eyebrows. "Where did he go?"

"Out toward the alpacas." A tickle drew her attention to her foot. After she brushed the ant away, she lifted her gaze and found Ryan headed in the same direction Basir had gone. She rolled her eyes and picked up her bucket. "Thanks for the help, Ryan. I really appreciate you picking up your friend's slack."

Meghan moved to the next row. Had it just been last weekend that the men had promised to take over some of the chores so she wouldn't be as overwhelmed with work? While they'd done a great job of helping out with the alpacas and the dishes, she really could have used the help with weeding today. It was a hot, dirty chore, and with the temperature rising, the work would soon go from tedious to miserable.

Once again, she felt the twang of guilt in her heart. With both guys acting strangely, she should be worried about them, not selfishly holding a one-person pity party. So what if she had to take care of the garden on her own? She was perfectly capable of doing it. What she should be doing instead of whining to herself was praying for her brother and his friend. Both men had endured things she couldn't even begin to imagine. Chances were, memories of those things had come to mind for Basir and rendered him unable to follow through on his promise. If that was the case, he would need Ryan's support to help him through it.

Meghan paused and looked up at the cloudless sky. "Father, forgive my selfish, self-centered thoughts. Please be with Basir and help him through whatever is going on. And, Lord, please give Ryan the wisdom he needs to help his friend. They both need Your healing touch, and I trust You to do whatever is best for them."

Peace settled over her, and she leaned down to pluck another weed from the warm earth.

~*~

Basir stared across the pasture and listened to

Ryan's familiar footfalls approach. He kept his gaze on the alpacas, struggling to keep his temper under control as his friend leaned against the fence beside him.

"Hey, weren't you supposed to help Meghan in the garden this morning?"

"Yes." Basir clenched his jaw, wishing Ryan would quit acting as if everything was all right.

"So, why are you out here instead of in the garden?"

Basir turned toward him and yanked off his sunglasses, squinting in the bright light as he glared. "How can you allow your sister to be seen like that?"

"Huh?" Confusion filled Ryan's face. "Seen like what?"

"Exposed! She is barely clothed, Ryan." Reason broke through his indignation, and he realized Meghan could have left the garden before her brother came out. "Did you not see her?"

"I saw her, but I don't know what you're talking—oh." Ryan looked up at the brilliant blue sky and combed his fingers through his hair. Then he met Basir's gaze again. "Look, man, you know things are different here. Meghan's shorts and shirt are considered modest."

"What!" Unable to stand the bright light searing into his sensitive eyes any longer, Basir put his sunglasses back on and gazed across the pasture as he tried to understand his friend's senseless words. "But her legs are bare, you can see to her shoulders, and her shape...it is not hidden at all. How can that be modest?"

Ryan scrubbed a hand across the back of his neck. "Haven't you seen what other American women wear?

Meghan's shirt covers her chest and her shorts come most of the way to her knees. That's very modest compared to what some women wear."

He had to admit his friend had a point. Unfortunately, Ryan didn't seem to understand Basir's point.

"Meghan is not some other woman. She is your sister." Basir lowered his head and his voice, praying his friend would not be angry when he added the real reason for his concern. "She is special."

Ryan studied him for uncomfortably long moments before finally speaking. "Yes, she is special, but we're in America, not Afghanistan. Meghan is free to make her own decisions regarding her clothing, and as I said, what she's currently wearing is modest."

"Aren't you afraid of how men will look at her? How they will treat her? Don't you want to protect her?" Perhaps he should have been more obvious when sharing his feelings about Meghan. He had fallen hard for her and wanted to protect her the only way he could—by ensuring her modesty and reputation remained intact. Surely her brother wanted the same things.

"Of course I want to protect her, but I can't force her to wear a burka. The men around here know her and respect her, Basir. They won't harm her."

Ryan's words finally soaked in, working their way past Basir's culturally induced indignation. He dropped his head to his hands as the reality of how much had changed when he left Afghanistan hit him like a mortar shell. Ashamed of his overreaction to something that no one in America viewed as an issue, he lowered his hands and kept his head down. He placed one hand over his heart, unable to meet Ryan's gaze.

"Forgive me, my friend. Things are so different here. I have learned much about American culture, especially since leaving Afghanistan, but so much of it goes against what I learned from my own family and community."

"There is nothing to forgive. You were only concerned for Meghan's reputation and safety. I understand that, and I appreciate you caring so much about her." Ryan gripped Basir's shoulder, the gesture full of brotherly affection. "Would it help to go talk to the pastor? Maybe he could help you figure out how to adjust to the differences between our worlds."

Basir nodded and straightened, grateful his friend remembered something of Afghan culture after all, even if it was only the importance of faith in everyday life. "The religious leaders always know the way things should be."

They headed back toward the house, side by side, and Basir wrestled with the two cultures warring in his mind. It seemed as if he could adjust to life in America without too much trouble, except for where Meghan was concerned. Something about her, or possibly his feelings for her, brought out his protective nature and his Afghan upbringing full force. No matter how hard he tried to convince himself that American cultural rules applied to her too, he couldn't get past feeling she was different. As he had told Ryan moments before, she was special. Unfortunately, he wasn't sure what to do about it.

Everything he knew about relationships with women came from the stories of the marines and his own observations and experience in his village. No way would he ever consider treating Meghan the way a few of the marines had mentioned. He had too much respect for her and viewed her as much more valuable than the objectified women those marines had told stories of. Other marines had spoken of relationships with wives and girlfriends, and though he appreciated their respect for the women in their lives, those stories didn't help him now when he was trying to figure out how to start a relationship. Yet what he had learned in his village didn't apply to her, either, which left him alone and adrift as he tried to figure out what he should do. If he wasn't afraid of offending Ryan by admitting to his attraction to Meghan, he would seek his friend's advice. But he couldn't bring himself to risk losing the closest thing he had to family.

As they approached the garden, he spotted Meghan standing with her hands on her hips, watching their progress. Basir's heart seized, and he wished he could disappear. How angry was she that he had broken his promise to assist her? Worse still, what would she think if she ever found out he had chosen not to help her because he thought her outfit immodest?

Looking at her now and comparing her to memories of other American women, he could see what Ryan had mentioned. When he considered some of the things he had seen women wearing since coming to the U.S., he knew without a doubt that Meghan's clothing—though revealing by Afghan standards—was undeniably modest. Somehow, he had to remember that regardless of his feelings for her, American culture applied at all times, not Afghan culture. He wasn't sure how to leave behind something so ingrained in him, however, and could only hope the minister would be able to help.

"So," Meghan said when they reached the garden, "are you guys going to help me?"

Ryan paused his steps. "Not right now. We're going into town for a little bit."

"Have fun." She blew out a breath that hung guilt heavily on Basir's heart.

It was his fault she didn't have the help he had promised, but perhaps he could make it up to her. "If you would like, we can finish weeding the garden for you when we return."

"It'll be too hot out here by the time you get back."

Ryan shrugged. "It's only going to be in the low nineties today. We've dealt with worse."

Basir prayed Meghan would accept his offer as she studied them. "Are you guys sure you want to pull weeds when it's that hot?"

"Yes." Basir spoke without hesitation and without checking with Ryan. He would do the weeding himself if he had to. "I promised I would help, and I will. I just can't do it immediately."

"All right." Meghan's smile made the coming sacrifice worth every bit of effort it would require. "I'll do a little more and then leave the rest for you guys."

Basir covered his heart with his right hand and then followed Ryan to his car. Perhaps Meghan hadn't been as angry as he'd feared. Or perhaps she was more understanding and forgiving than he had realized.

6

Basir stood beside Ryan in the church office and prayed he would have the strength to be honest with the pastor. He struggled with talking about his emotions, but thanks to his overreaction to Meghan's clothing, he didn't have much choice but to do it anyway. If he would have ignored his feelings for her and paid attention to what he knew of American ways, he would have been in the garden pulling weeds when Ryan found him.

His sigh brought Ryan's gaze to him. "Relax. You have to admit waiting here is better than some of the places we've waited."

Basir managed a faint smile. His friend made a valid point. At least they weren't stuck on the side of a dirt road in the middle of nowhere, the sun beating down on them while they waited for an ordnance disposal team to clear the way ahead.

A middle-aged man with brown hair just starting to show signs of gray stepped into the room. "Sorry to keep you waiting."

"It's no problem," Ryan said with a smile as they followed the pastor into his private office. As the pastor closed the door, Ryan clapped a hand to Basir's shoulder. "Basir, here, could use some advice."

"I'll do my best to provide it." The gentleman turned to Basir. "I saw you Sunday, but I didn't have a chance to introduce myself. I'm Joel Harte, the pastor here."

"I am Basir Hamidi, friend of Ryan and his sister." At least, he hoped he was her friend. After this morning, he couldn't be sure.

"He was an interpreter with my unit in Afghanistan," Ryan added.

"It's a pleasure to meet you." Joel shook Basir's hand and then studied him. "So, what is it you need advice on?"

Embarrassment flooded Basir at the prospect of admitting his overreaction to something so simple, so commonplace. Yet he had come to speak with the minister in an attempt to prevent such an overreaction in the future. Swallowing what little pride he had left intact, he met the pastor's gaze. "Clothing and American culture."

"Not the usual things people come to me for, but I'll do what I can." Pastor Joel lifted his hand toward a cluster of upholstered furniture. "Why don't we sit down and talk?"

Basir moved to the couch, but Ryan stayed by the door. "I'll leave you to talk. Basir, whenever you're finished, I'll be in the library. It's just down the hall and on the right."

A moment of anxiety hit as Ryan left the room, but then Basir realized it was actually a blessing not to have him listen in on the conversation. Now he could be open with the pastor without having to worry about offending his friend.

Once he sat on the couch and Joel settled in a facing chair, the pastor spoke. "I can tell you're nervous, Basir, but I don't bite. Whatever you say in here will be held in the strictest confidence."

"I appreciate that." He drew in a fortifying breath

and let it out with a sigh. "Ryan suggested I talk to you after I reacted badly to Meghan's clothing choice this morning."

"Why don't you tell me what happened?"

Basir briefly outlined the incident. "I know I am in America now and the rules from Afghanistan no longer apply, but that culture is a part of me. I don't know that I can leave it behind as easily as some may wish I could."

"That's perfectly understandable. You haven't been in the country long, have you?"

"I have been here for several months, but before I moved in with Ryan and his sister, I was mostly in hospitals. I was injured in an explosion, and the American government chose to bring me to the United States for treatment. They also gave me a green card for the service I did for them."

"Congratulations." Joel studied him again, and Basir had the uncanny feeling the man could read him as well as the local imam in the village where he had grown up. "So, this is really your first opportunity to experience normal American life."

Basir considered the statement. Outside of a few excursions to a store or a restaurant while he was rehabilitating, his only exposure to American culture had been on a military base in Afghanistan and in a medical setting. He doubted either place had provided an accurate example of what life in the United States was truly like. "Yes, that is correct."

"In that case, you need to go easy on yourself. It's clear you have learned quite a bit through your work with the marines and since coming here, but you can't reasonably expect to instantly adjust to life in a foreign country, especially one so different from your homeland."

"Yes, but it is more than just a difficulty adjusting to a vastly different culture." Basir looked down, praying for the strength to admit what he had yet to tell anyone else. "I don't know how to interact with women. Women I am attracted to, I mean. How to approach them, what is acceptable, what is not... these are things I have never had to worry about."

"Do you need to worry about them right now, or could you wait to think about dating until you've had time to adjust to your new life?"

"I must think about it now."

Joel smiled and leaned back in his chair. "I take it someone has caught your eye?"

"Yes, and I would like to know her, be friends with her, but I don't know how." Basir shook his head, feeling like a complete idiot. Even the eighteen-year-old marines he'd spoken to had more experience with women than he did, and they had never been married. "In Afghanistan, these things were never an issue. My father and my wife's father arranged our marriage. Dating was not allowed, and neither were casual friendships between single men and women. I never spent much time around the female marines, and even the hospital had male nurses and therapists."

"I see." The pastor appeared disconcerted, but he didn't leave Basir wondering for long. "You mentioned your marriage was arranged. Where is your wife now?"

"She is dead." A part of him shut down with the admission, numbing the pain of the memories and reminding him of one of the many reasons why he never talked about her.

"I'm sorry to hear that. It must be difficult to be

such a young widower."

The man had no idea. Basir nodded anyway, determined to bring the conversation back to his need for advice. "I want to become fully American, to have the same confidence I see in American men when they interact with women, but I don't know how to do that and still respect the women."

"Have you thought about asking Ryan to help you?"

"He just tells me to talk to women and let go of the cultural expectations that are holding me back. I know he means well, but it is not as easy for me as he thinks it should be."

"What about Meghan? Since you live on her farm, you must interact with her regularly. Perhaps with enough practice with her, you will be more comfortable interacting with other women."

Somehow, Basir doubted that would work any better than seeking Ryan's assistance. "Pastor, you must understand something. The way American women dress...it is very different from the way respectable women in my homeland dress. That is why I overreacted to what Meghan chose to wear this morning. If a woman dressed like that in Afghanistan—" He couldn't bring himself to bluntly speak the assumption about her morals that would be made. "Well, she might be approached by many men, but she would not be respected by them or anyone else."

"I think I'm beginning to understand your difficulty. When you see women dressed in such a manner, it's hard for you to remember that they deserve to be treated with respect, isn't it?"

Basir shook his head and fought down rising

anger at what the man implied about his own morals. "No. I try to respect all women, but when I see them dressed in such a way, I have to wonder about their reputations. I don't know which women have the same moral standards I do, and I don't want anything to do with an immoral woman. With Meghan, when I saw her shorts and shirt this morning, I worried how other men would see her, because I know she is a good woman with strong morals and a good reputation. However, her clothing makes it appear as though she is the opposite."

"Except that from what you have described, her clothing would convey the strong morals and good reputation to American men."

"That is why Ryan brought me here. I want protect Meghan's reputation and keep her safe from disreputable men, but the only way I know to do that would likely offend her."

"Didn't you say Ryan told you she is respected by the men in the community and therefore is safe?"

"Yes, but her clothing..." Basir shook his head, trying not to remember the desire that had flowed through him at the sight of her. "I have trouble believing God would approve."

"Let me show you something that may help ease your concerns." Joel stood and retrieved a leather-bound book from his desk. Instead of returning to his chair, he sat beside Basir on the couch and flipped through some pages. "The Bible doesn't give specific guidelines for acceptable clothing. The references are rather ambiguous in terms of style, but here is one verse I think you can agree Meghan's clothing followed. It's Deuteronomy chapter twenty-two, verse five. 'A woman must not wear men's clothing, nor a man wear women's clothing, for the Lord your God detests anyone who does this.'"

Basir turned the verse over in his mind and had to agree that Meghan had followed it. Her clothing had been undeniably feminine and designed for women.

"There are a pair of verses in First Timothy that may help as well." Joel flipped to the back half of his Bible. A moment later, he read, "Chapter two, verses nine and ten say, 'I also want the women to dress modestly, with decency and propriety, adorning themselves, not with elaborate hairstyles or gold or pearls or expensive clothes, but with good deeds, appropriate for women who profess to worship God.'"

Basir could agree that Meghan followed most of the direction, but one part was too vague to help. "What is modest dress that shows decency and propriety? Where I come from, it apparently means something very different than what it means here."

"And that, my friend, is where the cultural differences enter into it." Joel closed his Bible and laid it beside him. "You have told me that in Afghanistan Meghan's clothing would be considered immodest and revealing. But you're not in Afghanistan anymore. Think about what you have seen on other American women. How does Meghan's outfit compare to that?"

Considering how much skin he had seen since the weather warmed up, he could only give one answer. "Her clothing is modest compared to much of what I have seen."

"Which means she's following the biblical directive in First Timothy. Correct?" At Basir's nod, Pastor Joel smiled. "Recognizing that is the first step to adjusting to the cultural differences you're facing. Now you just have to remind yourself that because you are in a different country, the rules may be completely different than what you're used to. I know it's difficult, but you have to accept that the new rules are just as good and valid as the old. There's no way around it if you want to become fully American."

"I know." Although the pastor was telling him essentially the same things Ryan had been telling him all along, hearing it from a second person—and a religious leader, at that—drove home the point. No matter how uncomfortable it made him, he had to let go of his reservations and start acting like an American man, especially if he ever wanted to have a chance with Meghan.

~*~

Meghan turned off the burner under the dye pot and shoved a strand of hair out of her face. The guys had been gone for nearly two hours, and she was starting to worry. Basir had seemed so subdued, almost ashamed when they left. She couldn't figure out what could have happened to cause him to act so strangely, but now that he and her brother had been gone so long, she couldn't help wondering if something was seriously wrong.

She checked the yarn one more time and shook her head. Never had she imagined she would be asked to create almost fluorescent blue yarn, but unusual requests were a hazard of taking the occasional custom order. She stepped away from the stove and untied her apron. As she hung it on the hook by the door to her workshop, the front door opened. She stepped into the hallway as Ryan and Basir came in and closed the door.

Both men appeared much more relaxed than they had when they left, but Basir couldn't seem to look at her. She'd thought he was making progress in that area in the last few days, not counting the glances he regularly stole. But now he seemed to have regressed to looking everywhere but in her direction. She said a silent prayer for the strength to deal with whatever was going on.

"Sorry it took so long," Ryan said. "We'll head out to the garden now and deal with the weeds."

"Thanks." Meghan followed as they headed toward the back door. "I went ahead and finished half of it, since that's what I'd planned on doing anyway."

"OK." Ryan stopped by the stove and peered into the cooling pot. "I assume that's not lunch."

Basir gave him a questioning look and joined him at the stove. Meghan laughed at their doubtful expressions as they took in the almost clear liquid with bright blue yarn floating in it.

"It would give you a lot of fiber, but no. That's some yarn someone ordered." She studied the yarn. "I wasn't sure about the color at first, but I think it's starting to grow on me."

"It sure is bright." Ryan shook his head and moved toward the back door. "Come on, Basir. Let's finish the garden before it gets any hotter out there."

Meghan watched them head outside, and then she went to her workshop. With Basir's silence and the strange way the day had gone so far, her thoughts were a whirl of chaos. Spinning yarn always helped her focus and clear her mind. She had a feeling that calm and clear-headed would be essential to helping Basir adjust to life in America. Now if she could just find a way to help him get past his fear of talking to her or whatever it was that held him back. The little she had managed to learn about him only made her more curious, and she couldn't deny finding him attractive.

Ryan drifted through her mind, and she wondered what he would think if he knew she was interested in his friend. Then again, Ryan had brought Basir into the house in the first place and encouraged Meghan to befriend the man. He would probably approve of a relationship between them, if their friendship ever made it past the fledgling stage.

By the time she heard the back door open and close, she had produced several yards of yarn and found the peace she'd hoped for. She adjusted the yarn so it wouldn't untwist and went to the kitchen.

Ryan stood at the sink draining a glass of water. He swallowed the last of it and faced her. "Garden's done. Basir insisted on checking the alpacas and making sure they have plenty of clean water before he comes in."

"I'll have to be sure to thank him for thinking of the herd." Meghan moved to the cabinet and pulled out a pitcher. "Would you guys prefer iced tea or lemonade?"

"I could go either way, and Basir will accept anything you offer." Ryan chuckled and set his glass in the sink. "It would be rude of him to refuse."

"No, it wouldn't."

"Sure it would. At least it would be where he comes from." He shook his head with a reminiscent expression. "I can't believe the amount of tea I drank in the process of trying to gain the trust of the locals. There were times I thought I'd float if I had to look at another glass of tea."

Meghan smiled, thankful her brother had mentioned something about his time in Afghanistan. Usually he avoided all mention of it or walked off as soon as he said anything about it. Maybe having Basir stay with them was the catalyst he needed to finally heal.

"If you drank that much tea," she said, "maybe Basir would prefer iced tea."

"Go with whatever sounds good to you. I happen to know he likes lemonade as well as tea."

Meghan considered for a moment then retrieved a second pitcher. "I'll make both, and then people can drink whatever they want."

"You and your diplomacy." Ryan laughed and moved aside as she stepped to the sink. "Or are you just indecisive?"

She grinned and set the pitchers on the counter. "I think I'll go with the diplomacy. It sounds so much better."

Basir came into the kitchen as Meghan pulled sandwich ingredients out of the refrigerator. Lunch was quiet but comfortable, and Meghan lost some of her earlier concern. Although Basir was still a little more subdued than he had been the day before, he seemed more peaceful than when he and Ryan went into town. When he gave her a small smile as she refilled his glass with lemonade, hope rose that their fledgling friendship hadn't crashed and burned after all.

After lunch, Ryan announced he would be back in time for dinner and went out the front door. Basir seemed uncomfortable at first, but he stayed in the kitchen while Meghan cleaned up from lunch, giving her the courage to speak what had been on her mind for the last few hours.

She set the last dish in the drainer on the counter and returned to her seat at the table. "Basir, can I ask you something?"

His expression grew guarded. "I suppose so."

"What happened this morning? I mean, why did you walk off instead of coming to the garden?"

He remained silent long enough to make her wonder if she should have held her tongue. Then he spoke quietly, his gaze on the table top. "I guess you could say I forgot how to deal with American culture. I made a bad assumption, but I have since corrected my thinking."

She studied him for a moment but the confusion remained. "I don't understand."

"Where I come from, respectable women do not wear clothing like yours." Basir briefly met her gaze and looked away again. "Here, respectable women do wear clothing like yours. I still have a lot of adjusting to do since your culture is much different from the one I grew up in."

"My clothing is what upset you?" Memories flashed of news reports showing women clad in long dresses with long sleeves, their heads covered. "I'm sorry I made you uncomfortable."

"You have nothing to apologize for." Basir shifted in his seat and looked at her a little longer before his eyes moved away once more. "I am the one who should apologize for overreacting to something that needed no reaction at all."

"Like you said, you have a lot of adjusting to do." Although she was sure her brother would doubt the wisdom of what she was about to do, she couldn't ignore that pesky nudge in her heart. "I can easily wear different clothes if it would make that adjustment easier for you. I'm sure it still won't be like what you're used to, but maybe it would help a little."

Basir stared at her, his eyes wide. "You would do that for me?"

"Yes. I want you to be comfortable here."

"But would you be comfortable?"

"I plan on wearing things that I find comfortable. Maybe a long skirt instead of shorts?"

Although he looked as if he wanted to agree, he slowly shook his head. "I can't ask you to change what you normally wear. I am a guest in your house, and I have no right to ask anything of you anyway."

"You're not asking me to do anything." Meghan could see his stubborn nature wouldn't back down, so she made a quick decision. "Wait here for a minute, OK? I'll be right back."

She hurried upstairs and dug through a dresser drawer until she found the ankle-length skirt she was looking for. A moment later, she'd exchanged it for her shorts. The lightweight material flowed around her legs as she headed back to the kitchen. Regardless of whether Basir appreciated her clothing change, she liked the way the skirt felt. It was light and loose enough to keep her cool in the mid-summer heat, and it was long enough that no one could argue over its modesty.

When she stepped into the kitchen, Basir's expression made her question whether she had truly made the right decision. His eyes widened, but he looked away before she could decipher the emotions roiling in the tawny-brown depths. She hesitantly stepped closer to where he still sat at the table.

Clasping her hands in front of her waist, she tried

to quell her nerves. "Will clothing like this make it easier for you to talk to me and adjust to life here?"

He slowly rose from his seat, his gaze nowhere near her face. "You did not have to change for me."

"I know, but I want you to be comfortable around me." She bit her lip and looked down as she fought the urge to cry. Had she made the situation worse by trying to help?

"I'm trying, but it is difficult regardless of what you wear." Basir stepped closer. "You do look beautiful in that skirt, though."

Her eyes darted up and met his. Maybe she had done the right thing after all. The warmth in his expression confirmed her suspicion that he was attracted to her, and the way he moved to stand directly in front of her gave her hope that maybe their friendship would grow stronger. Her pulse increased as she realized he stood closer to her now than he ever had, even though it was still farther away than many of the men Julia had set her up with.

Basir reached out and brushed his fingers across the back of her hand, sending fireworks exploding through her. "Thank you for caring so much about a man you barely know."

He touched me.

The thought bounced around her brain, rendering her temporarily incapable of speech. How could one simple skirt bring about such a change in the man who had essentially avoided her since moving in? Better yet, why hadn't she thought to wear long skirts before now?

The uncertainty in his features brought her out of her thoughts, and she smiled. "It's easy to care about you."

His face flushed as he dropped his gaze to the floor, and her heart did a happy dance. Seeing evidence that her words affected him gave her a sense of power, but it also made her feel closer to him somehow. Almost as though what she said mattered to him on a deeper level than she'd realized.

Aware of how difficult it was for him to be so sociable with her, she decided to give him an easy out. "I need to get the yarn out of the dye pot and hang it up to dry."

"Do you need help with it?" He sounded puzzled as he glanced at the pot still sitting on the stove.

"Not really. I just need to squeeze out most of the water then take the yarn outside and hang it on the porch."

He nodded and looked at her long enough to give her a brief smile that made her feel a little giddy. "Then I think I will go clean the alpacas' pasture."

Meghan watched him head outside and smiled. Maybe she would get the chance to find out her brother's opinion of her having a relationship with Basir after all.

E. A. West

7

A shout startled Meghan awake, and she sat up, the covers sliding to her lap. Had something happened to the alpacas? The house couldn't be on fire since the smoke detectors were silent. Another shout broke the quiet of the night, and footsteps raced down the hall. As they passed her door it finally sank in that the shouts were coming from the direction of Basir's room. Her brother was responsible for the footsteps.

Meghan threw back the covers and hurried into the hall, praying Basir was OK. Muffled voices drifted out of his room as she approached, and her heart nearly broke as she caught part of the conversation.

"...nothing for me there."

"I know." Her brother's voice held a soothing tone. "But you've got a place here, now. Meghan and I both think of you as family. You're not alone."

"But Meghan doesn't know... She can't understand what it was like. The bombs, the gunfire, the fear..." Basir's voice broke.

"She may not understand, but she cares. She knows you're having a rough time, just like I did when I first got here."

"But even you don't understand. You didn't have your own people try to kill you."

Meghan peeked through the open door and found Ryan sitting on the edge of Basir's bed. Basir had his knees pulled up to his chest and his arms wrapped around his legs. Despair filled his features as he looked at Ryan. "You did not lose your family because you chose to help the United States."

"No, but I know what went on over there. I know what you went through. Just because I wasn't the target doesn't mean I don't understand. Not after everything you and I went through together. Didn't I keep you from bleeding out when you were attacked in that village? Didn't I help you when you first found out your family disowned you?"

Basir nodded, his gaze downcast. "You are right. Forgive me."

"There's nothing to forgive, my brother." Ryan rested a hand on his friend's shoulder. "You'll get through this just like you've gotten through everything else. I'm here for you, and so is Meghan. You can trust her just as much as you trust me."

Her brother's insistence that she was trustworthy made her heart twist with guilt. Here she stood, eavesdropping on a private conversation. Even though she'd only come out of concern for Basir, she should have gone back to her room the moment she heard the men talking. Heat flooded her face, and she backed away from the door. The quiet murmur of male voices continued behind her as she reached her room and stepped inside.

Once she closed the door, she leaned back against the wood and closed her eyes.

"Forgive me, Father," she whispered. She released her guilt on the wings of prayer, and the weight lifted from her soul.

She climbed back in bed and settled under the covers, but she couldn't quiet her mind enough to fall asleep. Worry kept up a constant tornado of questions.

What had caused Basir to shout? Would talking to Ryan do enough to help him? What could she do to help him heal from whatever he had been through?

What *had* he been through?

That was the biggest question looming in her mind. What little she'd heard told her he had been through much more than either he or her brother had even hinted at. She longed to understand what life had been like for him in Afghanistan so that she could help him heal and adjust to a safe life in the United States, but the small bits of information the men had revealed made her wonder if she really wanted to know more.

Each time Ryan had been deployed, she'd carried around a constant fear that something terrible would happen to him. In her weakest moments, she'd been terrified her twin would come home in a casket. In all the e-mails he'd sent and the phone calls they'd shared while he was in Afghanistan, he'd never once hinted at how much danger he'd truly been in. He plied her with humorous anecdotes about the guys in his unit, locals he'd witnessed, and the contents of MREs he had eaten. She'd known even then that he was holding back a lot to protect her, and she'd been thankful. Then he had come home and moved into her house.

From his first night on the farm, his actions had made it clear that he had numerous memories that weighed heavily on his mind. Meghan had never asked him for details, and he hadn't offered any. She'd assumed he would eventually work through everything and either tell her about some of it or put it all behind him and move on with his life. Although it felt a little like hiding her head in the sand to pretend things couldn't have been too bad for him while on deployment, it kept her calm and helped relieve the worry about her brother.

Now, however, she couldn't help wondering if the rose-colored glasses approach had been a mistake. The longer Basir lived with them, the more obvious it became that Ryan harbored a lot of memories that were likely to haunt him for the rest of his life, including some that would traumatize even the most stoic marine. What man wouldn't be deeply affected by having to keep his close friend from bleeding to death?

Meghan's eyes stung as she realized how little she knew about her twin, the guy she'd been closer to than anyone else for their entire lives. Then there was Basir. How could she ever hope to get to know him when there was so much about his life before coming to the United States that she couldn't possibly understand?

"Oh, Lord, help me know what to do," she whispered as the tears slipped past her lashes. "I care so much about both of them, but I have no idea what to do for them. Please guide me in my interactions with them and give me the wisdom I need to strengthen the relationships I have with them. And, Father, please heal them both. I have no doubt they need You to get past whatever they went through over there. Give them the strength to face whatever ghosts have followed them here and help them find their way free of those memories so they can live happy, successful lives as civilians."

She rolled onto her side and dried her eyes as her heart continued the prayer. No more words came to mind, but she knew God would understand. The book of Romans promised the Holy Spirit would intercede for her.

Her tumultuous thoughts gradually calmed, and she thanked God for bringing peace to her mind and heart. She closed her eyes and had just started to doze off when she heard a light tap on her door.

"Megs?" Ryan's soft voice barely reached her ears. "You awake?"

"Yeah." She opened her eyes and sat up. "Come on in."

The door swung open, and her brother entered the room. He sat on the foot of her bed and combed his fingers through his messy hair. Then he looked at her. Even in the darkness broken only by the light of the moon and the stars coming through the window, she could see he was troubled.

"I know you heard some of what Basir and I talked about." He sighed and lowered his head. "I didn't want you to know how bad it was when I was over there, but maybe I should have told you more."

Meghan scooted closer and laid her hand on his shoulder, wishing she'd never eavesdropped. "I didn't hear much."

"You heard enough, I'm sure." Ryan shook his head and met her gaze. "He and I both have a lot of stuff that will stay with us forever. He's got more, which I'm sure you already realized."

"I wish I knew what to do to help you guys deal with it."

"Keep doing what you have been." Ryan wrapped her in a hug. "I can never thank you enough for giving me a safe place to readjust to life. I know Basir feels the same way."

"I'm just glad I had a place to give you." Meghan sat back and brushed a strand of hair away from her eyes. "Don't take this the wrong way, but would it help if you talked to a counselor?"

"Yes, it would. It does." Ryan offered a sheepish

smile. "I probably should have mentioned it before, but I've been seeing a guy at the VA outpatient clinic for a couple of months."

"You don't have to tell me everything." Meghan gave him another hug. "I'm glad it helps, though."

"Me too."

She released her brother as she considered how to ask her next question. Straightforward seemed like the best approach. "Has Basir thought about talking to a counselor?"

"Not until I suggested it to him tonight. I'm taking him to the clinic tomorrow to get him signed up." Ryan stood and then reached down and tugged a strand of her hair. "We'll all get through this and figure out what we're doing eventually. Just don't let Basir know you overheard anything tonight. He didn't see you in the doorway like I did, and I'm not sure how well it would go over."

"I didn't mean to overhear anything. I just wanted to make sure everything was OK."

"I know." He smiled and headed for the door. "Sleep well…for what's left of the night."

"You too." She watched him step into the hall and close the door, and then she flopped back on her pillow and attempted to go back to sleep.

~*~

Morning arrived far too early in Basir's opinion. The nightmares the night before had made it nearly impossible to sleep, and when he did it was far from restful. His head throbbed as he pulled on jeans and a T-shirt and headed downstairs. He didn't hold out much hope for a good day and prayed Meghan wouldn't be offended if he avoided her and the rest of the world. Dealing with someone as kind and wonderful as Meghan was more than he could handle after a night of dreams about his wife's death and the destruction of his honor. She deserved much better than him, but he didn't know how to let go of his fragile hope that maybe one day he could have a relationship with her.

He paused at the base of the stairs and rubbed his temples. The motion did nothing to relieve his headache, so he dropped his hands to his sides and headed back upstairs to grab the medication a doctor had prescribed for his migraines. When he finally reached the kitchen, prescription bottle in hand, Meghan and Ryan both sat at the table. They greeted him with smiles he couldn't return as he headed for the cabinet.

"Everything OK?" Ryan asked.

Basir pulled out a glass and resisted the urge to shake his head. "Migraine."

"I'm sorry to hear that."

The sympathy in his friend's voice made him sigh. As much as he appreciated Ryan loving him like a brother, this morning Basir couldn't bring himself to believe he was worth it. How could anyone have concern for a man who had failed to protect his wife and had been disowned by his family? He had nothing, was nothing.

And yet...

He swallowed the pill and drank a little more water as his mind raced. Ryan had never shown him anything but kindness and respect. Even when he was at his worst, when his honor was completely destroyed, Ryan had continued to treat him like a brother. Then, he had come here, broken and with permanent injuries, and Meghan had welcomed him with open arms. She had gone out of her way to make him comfortable and to help him adjust to a new way of life. Just last week she had voluntarily changed her clothes to make him more comfortable.

Maybe he was worth having someone care about him after all. Maybe his honor wasn't as unredeemable as he had assumed. Perhaps instead of looking at the past and worrying about everything he had done wrong, he needed to look forward and realize that with a different society came different expectations. According to Ryan, he was a good man and worthy of respect. If an all-American marine believed that about him, perhaps it was time to accept that it could be true.

Basir set his glass on the counter beside his pill bottle and turned around. The sympathy and concern in Meghan's eyes warmed his heart and increased his determination to try to see himself as worthy.

"Would you like me to fix you some breakfast?" she asked, her soft voice soothing his frayed nerves.

"Yes, please." Surprisingly, his headache hadn't killed his appetite yet. He didn't hold out much hope for the coming hours, but perhaps he had taken his medication soon enough that it would keep the worst of the migraine away.

She rose from her seat. "What would you like?"

"Anything is fine." He had no doubt she would prepare anything he asked for, but he didn't want to impose upon her hospitality.

She studied him for a moment, and then turned to her brother. "Do you have any preferences?"

"Whatever you want to fix is fine with me."

"Pancakes and scrambled eggs it is, then." She

returned her gaze to Basir. "Why don't you go ahead and sit down?"

"I should feed the alpacas."

"I already did it," Ryan said and grinned. "I figured you could use the break this morning."

"Thank you. I appreciate it." Basir sank into a chair at the table and rested his head in his hands. The spear still pierced his skull, making him even more grateful his friend had cared for the herd. With the way he felt right now, he wasn't sure he could manage to feed and water the alpacas and let them out into the pasture for the day.

His mind wandered as Meghan moved around the kitchen, and he remembered Ryan mentioning counseling the night before. He had been resistant to the idea at first, but then Ryan had admitted to his own need for counseling. If his friend thought it was a good idea and effective in helping one adjust to normal life, perhaps he should give it a try as well. Not only did he have many memories that wouldn't let him go, but he also needed help figuring out how to live as an American man. The pastor had provided useful advice, yet Basir still felt he needed more. Someone who could offer guidance when necessary and assist him in putting the past behind him would undoubtedly be valuable.

Meghan set a plate of food in front of him and another in front of her brother. "Do you guys want orange juice?"

"I'll get it, Megs," Ryan said as he stood. "You get your own breakfast and sit down."

"Yes, sir." Her laugh lightened the atmosphere of the room as she headed for the stove.

Ryan grinned and turned to Basir. "You want

orange juice?"

"Sure." He watched Meghan out of the corner of his eye. What would she think if he sought counseling? Would she approve, or would she think he was weak?

Throughout the meal, Basir's thoughts whirled around his aching head in a dizzying mess. One minute he thought he might be worthy of Meghan. The next he was certain he wasn't worthy of any woman, let alone one as wonderful as Meghan. He went back and forth on whether counseling was a good idea as well.

By the time he finished eating, he had decided the worst that could happen if he talked to a counselor was that he wasted his time. He still hadn't decided if he could ever be considered worthy of his best friend's sister. All he knew was that at some point he would have to either attempt to form a romantic relationship with her or move far away and never see her again. The latter option might be the best, but he couldn't bring himself to give it serious consideration. Not when he felt led deep in his heart to be near her.

As Meghan rose to clear the table, Ryan met Basir's gaze. "You up to getting out of here for a while?"

Basir knew his friend wanted to take him to the clinic for counseling. The dull throb in his skull wasn't likely to get better if he stayed at the farm, so there wasn't any point to delaying the trip. "Yes."

"Let's go, then." Ryan led the way out of the kitchen and stopped by the stairs. "You probably ought to grab that folder with all your papers in it. They'll require at least some of that information during the check-in process."

Basir nodded and went upstairs for the file folder

containing his important documents. Now that counseling was becoming a reality, anxiety hit. What if they told him they couldn't do anything for him? When he had gone to the neurologist, full of hope for a complete recovery, he had received the news that he would never recover to the way he was before the explosion. His brain had suffered permanent damage that might improve with time, but the damage would always be there.

Once he sat in the passenger seat of Ryan's car and they were on the road, he turned to his friend. "You are sure this is a good idea?"

"Yes." Ryan glanced at him before returning his gaze to the road. "Remember what I said last night? Getting into counseling was the best thing I've done since moving in with Meghan. It's helped me deal with the things I couldn't move past, the things that were holding me back."

"But you come from a culture where talking about the way you feel is common." Basir shook his head and looked out the window. "I don't know if I can tell a stranger about the things I have been through and what they have done to me."

"You don't have to tell the therapist everything in your first session. They expect you to hold stuff back until you get to know them and trust them. I think if you'll give them a chance, they'll be able to help you."

"Maybe." Another concern sprang to mind, one that almost made him change his mind about going. "You said you talked to a woman the first time you went."

"I did, but that was just for the intake. They assigned me to a man for my regular sessions."

Basir remained quiet, unsure if his friend

understood his concern. He didn't want to come right out and ask if there was a way to ensure he only had to speak with a man. Too many times already he had made it clear that he was a foreigner in this land. It was something that would have to be addressed at some point, however. Talking to another man would be difficult enough. No way could he bring himself to admit anything to a woman.

"We'll be sure to tell them you would prefer to speak with a male counselor," Ryan said, his voice filled with understanding. "They'll do their best to make the process as painless as possible, which for you means ensuring a man does your intake and subsequent counseling."

At least he wouldn't have to show his vulnerability to a strange woman. If he was going to show vulnerability to any woman, he wanted it to be Meghan. With her sweet nature, he had a feeling she would do her best to help him heal. He just had to find the courage to open himself up to her. Now that he thought about it, opening up to her might require less courage than telling Ryan how he felt about her.

The community-based outpatient clinic was about half an hour away from Meghan's farm. Inside, the receptionist handed Basir a stack of forms and a pen and instructed him to bring them back once he'd filled them out. He followed Ryan to a vacant corner of the waiting room and sat down with a sigh.

"I can't read these. Not today." Just the thought made his head pound harder.

Ryan sat in the chair beside him. "Don't worry about it. I'll fill them out. You just have to answer the questions I read to you."

Basir handed over the papers and pen, relieved he

didn't have to try to do it himself. If he did, it could take days to finish. As it was, with Ryan's help, it took less than half an hour to answer the seemingly endless list of questions. He leaned his head back against the wall and closed his eyes, giving them a rest from the constant burn of the lights overhead. Apparently, today's migraine had decided to make his eyes more light sensitive than usual.

"You want me to take these up to the receptionist for you?" Ryan asked.

Torn between resting and responsibility, he settled on resting. "Yes, please."

"OK. Be right back."

The sounds of the other people in the waiting room faded into the background as Basir breathed deeply in an attempt to relax. *Father God, help me through this. I can't do it alone.*

The simple prayer repeated itself over and over while he waited for Ryan's return. The mantra soothed his frayed nerves and helped him believe he could survive talking to a stranger about things he had trouble discussing with his best friend. Or perhaps it was God taking the burden from his shoulders and giving him the strength to face whatever lay ahead.

Someone sat down beside him, and he opened his eyes to find Ryan watching him.

"They'll call your name just as soon as someone is free to talk to you. When I mentioned that you'd prefer talking to a man, the receptionist said she would put a note in your file and see to it."

"Thank you, my friend." Basir managed a small smile, despite his continued apprehension about the upcoming intake session. At least he could lay one worry to rest.

~*~

"How did it go?" Ryan asked as Basir joined him.

"I have an appointment next week with the same man." Basir lifted a hand to indicate they could go. As they left the clinic, he continued. "After we talked, he agreed it would be better for me to continue to see him rather than have to start over with someone new as my regular counselor."

"Good! I told you they'd make the process as painless as possible." Ryan waited until they were in his car to speak again. "So, do you think this guy's going to help you?"

"Maybe. He is willing to listen to what I have to say, and he seems to understand that I need someone who can help me figure out how to adapt to American culture without completely losing myself."

"Hmm...I hadn't thought about it like that before." After a quiet moment, Ryan said, "Is that how you feel? Like if you accept American culture and become a part of it that you'll lose yourself?"

"A little. Things are so different here, and the way I was raised to believe and think is not always appreciated. But those ways are a part of me. I cannot leave them completely behind and still be me. On the other hand, I can't hold on to them so tightly and still become American."

"When you put it like that, I see how difficult the adjustment is for you."

Basir wasn't sure his friend would ever be able to understand the difficulties he faced, but he appreciated the attempt. It was more than many people did.

"While we're on the topic of you adjusting to life

here, how's it going with Meghan?"

The air left the car, and Basir stared at his friend. "What do you mean?"

"I know you've been trying to become friends with her. I was wondering how that's going. Is it getting easier for you to talk to her?"

"Some." Relief made it difficult to think. He really needed to talk to Ryan about his sister, but he was too afraid of damaging their friendship to risk it yet. "She is very patient and willing to do whatever she can to help me feel more comfortable."

"Is that why she's been wearing more long skirts and jeans instead of shorts?"

"Yes." Heat flooded his face at the memory of his discussion with her the day he'd overreacted to her outfit. "She cornered me into explaining that her clothing made me uncomfortable that day in the garden. I didn't ask her to change what she wears. She volunteered to do it despite me telling her she didn't need to."

Ryan laughed. "That sounds like my sister. I sometimes think her goal in life is to help as many people as she can."

"She is a good woman." Basir dug deep and found the courage to broach the subject that weighed so heavily on his heart and mind. "She will make a good wife someday."

"I'm sure she will, if she ever finds the right man."

As much as Basir wanted to believe he was that man, he knew too much stood in his way. It didn't diminish his hope, however, that he might have a chance with Meghan.

8

Basir stopped the lawnmower and wiped sweat from his brow. At least it was cloudy, so he didn't have to deal with the sun beating down on him and burning into his eyes. He hadn't realized how hard mowing the grass between the house and the street would be. According to Ryan, using the riding lawnmower made the task easier, but Basir had to use a push mower because the riding mower had gone in for repairs a few days ago. He would have volunteered even if he had known using the push mower would be so difficult. Meghan's smile was worth every bit of effort.

He reached for the pull cord to restart the mower, but a small sound stopped him. He straightened and looked toward the road, but he didn't see anything. The sound came again, the quiet mewling of a young animal. Unable to ignore it, he headed for the street, scanning the grass for the source of the sound. He finally found it in the ditch at the edge of the road.

A small, dirty cardboard box sat in a patch of knee-high weeds. The mewling sounds definitely came from inside. Basir knelt and lifted one of the torn flaps of the box. Inside rested four tabby kittens that were too young to be away from their mother. Two of them weren't moving at all. One was struggling to breathe, and the fourth wobbled around, calling in its tiny voice.

"Oh, you poor babies." Basir reached into the box

and ran a finger along the two kittens that weren't moving. Neither was breathing, and both were cold and stiff. Anger filled him that someone would abandon such young animals to die, but the mewing of the healthiest kitten broke through and he shoved the emotion aside. The two that still lived needed his care right now. He carefully lifted them from the box and tucked them into the hammock he made of his T-shirt by pulling up the hem. No way could he leave them with their dead littermates a moment longer. He stood and hurried toward the house, determined to do everything he could to help the kittens survive.

Ryan came in from the barn as Basir pulled the milk from the refrigerator. He opened his mouth to speak, but a particularly loud mew cut him off.

"What was that?" Ryan asked, stepping closer.

"A kitten." Basir set the milk on the counter and shifted the hem of his shirt aside to reveal the wretched creatures. "There were two more, but they were already dead when I found them."

"Where are they now?" Ryan asked as he moved to a cabinet and retrieved a small bowl.

"In a box in the ditch by the road." Basir watched his friend pour a small amount of milk in the bowl and carry it toward the microwave. "These two are too young to drink from a bowl."

Ryan paused and glanced at him over his shoulder. "How are you planning to give them the milk, then?"

"I can dip the corner of a cloth in it and let them suck on that until I can get them a bottle. Unless there is a bottle around here small enough for them?"

"No, we'll have to go into town for one." Ryan set the bowl in the microwave and turned it on. "There are dishcloths in that drawer by the sink."

Basir went to the indicated drawer and pulled out one of the folded cloths. By the time he settled in a chair at the table, Ryan had brought the warmed milk over and set it in front of him.

"Anything else I can do to help?"

Basir looked up at him. "Get another cloth and feed the noisy kitten. I will try to feed the other one, but I'm afraid it may not survive."

Within seconds, Ryan had retrieved a second dishcloth and dropped into the chair beside Basir. He accepted the healthier kitten and dipped a corner of the cloth in the milk. Basir scooped up the ill kitten and did the same.

After a few moments, Ryan's charge eagerly sucked the milk. Basir wished he was having as much luck. Unfortunately, the kitten appeared too weak to suckle a bit of cloth. He set it aside and dipped his index finger into the milk. The kitten showed a little more life when he let the milk drip on its mouth, but he held little hope for its recovery. It was just too weak to survive. He had to do everything he could for it, however.

By the time the kitten Ryan held was sated, the kitten in Basir's care had given up on eating and fallen asleep. Its labored breathing concerned Basir, and he looked at Ryan.

"This little one is not well."

Ryan nodded and stroked the one he held. "This one seems to be OK, at least for the moment. We should take them to the vet, though, and get them checked out."

Basir rose and shifted the kitten in his hands. It was so tiny, so fragile. The kitten clung to its life, but only barely. His heart broke at the thought of the kitten Ryan carried being left as the only survivor. It would need extra love and care to ensure it grew into a healthy, happy cat.

Ryan led the way through the house and out to his car. Basir settled into the passenger seat and laid the sickly kitten in his lap. He accepted the other one from his friend and laid it against its littermate, praying that small contact would be enough to help the sickly one. Ryan settled behind the wheel and started the engine.

"After we get back, I'll find that box you mentioned and take care of the dead ones. Meghan doesn't need to see them. She's got such a soft heart."

Basir lifted his gaze from the kittens in his lap, worry filling him. "Will she find them before we get back?"

"I doubt it. She was planning to be gone all afternoon, remember? We should have plenty of time to get these little guys checked out and get back before she shows up."

Basir nodded and stroked the tiny furry bodies. He hoped she wouldn't mind him taking care of the kittens. As Ryan had said, she had a soft heart. Basir could only pray that she would understand his need to care for the abandoned kittens.

The vet at the edge of town didn't offer much hope. "Well, there's a chance this one will survive with the right care, but this other one... I'm afraid its chances of survival are nonexistent. The poor thing is too weak and malnourished to recover."

Basir looked at the kitten struggling to draw in a breath, his mind going back to Afghanistan. He remembered his grandfather saying something similar about a lamb that had been abandoned by its mother.

Once its breathing grew too labored, his grandfather had shot it in the head to put it out of its misery.

"What do you recommend?" Ryan asked.

"Euthanasia for this one," the vet said as he stroked the prominent ribcage of the sickly kitten. "It's the most merciful thing you can do for it."

Basir nodded and picked up the other kitten, cradling it against his chest as he stroked its thin body. "This one, though, can live."

"Right. You'll need kitten formula, and you'll have to bottle feed it every two hours around the clock."

"Where can we get that?" Ryan asked.

"The feed store carries the formula and the bottles." The vet looked at the kitten still lying on the cold steel table. "Do you want to stay here while I put this one down?"

Even as Ryan shook his head, Basir spoke. "I will stay. Even though it will not live much longer, it should know that it was not abandoned a second time."

Ryan laid a hand on his shoulder. "You're a good man, Basir."

The vet nodded his agreement. "It will be over soon for the poor little guy. I'll go get the necessary supplies."

Once he left the room, Ryan studied Basir. "You mind if I go get the formula and bottle while he does whatever it is he needs to do? I'd rather not be witness to that poor thing's end, but I can hang around here if you want me to."

"Go get what this one needs," Basir said, stroking the kitten curled up in his hand. "I think you need to not be here as much as I need to stay."

"Probably. I'll be back as soon as I can. If you get

done here before I get back, just wait in the waiting room." Ryan left the exam room, and Basir reached down to pet the kitten lying on the table.

"Soon you will suffer no more," he whispered, unsure if it was even aware of his presence. "Know that you have at least one person who cared about you and will be sad when you are gone."

He continued to pet the kitten's worn body until the vet returned. The man worked efficiently, explaining the process of giving the kitten an overdose of anesthetic to end its life painlessly. Basir wasn't sure he wanted that much detail, but he had a feeling the vet wanted to talk to cover his own sadness at having to put down such a young creature. If only the owners had taken responsibility for their cat's litter, it never would have come to this. Basir felt renewed anger at the situation, but he was wise enough to realize he would likely never know who had abandoned such defenseless creatures.

Finally, the kitten's breathing stopped altogether, and the vet put on a stethoscope to check it. He shook his head as he removed the stethoscope. "At least it's not suffering anymore."

Basir nodded and held his hand out to the man. "Thank you for carrying out the task with compassion."

The vet shook his hand, looking a little surprised. "It's the least I can do in a difficult situation like this. The little one you're holding should be all right once he gains a little more weight. Regular feedings will help with that. Be sure to keep the little guy warm and rub him every now and then with a washcloth to simulate the mother's tongue."

"I will. Will you need me to bring him back here?"

"He'll need his kitten shots in a few weeks, but as long as he's doing all right, I shouldn't need to see him before then. You're welcome to call or come in if you have any questions, however."

"Thank you."

The vet glanced at the tiny furry body on the examining table. "I'd better take care of this little guy. The receptionist will have your bill ready for you in a few minutes."

"Thank you." Basir laid his hand over his heart and bowed his head, then he straightened and left the room.

Two people had arrived with their pets, and they watched Basir as he went to a chair against the wall and sat down. He smoothed the kitten and tucked him into the edge of his T-shirt while he tried to ignore the curious expressions of the two women. One had a plastic carrier holding a fluffy white cat. The other held the leash of a small dog lying in her lap.

The one with the cat broke the silence. "That kitten you have there seems rather young."

"It is about three weeks old." Basir risked glancing at her, but quickly looked away again. "Someone abandoned it on my friend's farm."

"Oh, my," the woman with the dog said. "You're not from around here, are you?"

"Not originally, no." Basir glanced out the window overlooking the parking lot and hoped Ryan would return soon.

"Where are you from?"

"Afghanistan." He sighed when the woman gasped. Maybe if he volunteered a little information, she wouldn't ask any stupid questions. "I was an interpreter for the Americans."

His plan failed. She placed a hand at her throat and stared at him. "So, you're not one of those Taliban people we hear such terrible things about?"

"No, I am not a Talib. I risked my life to help the Americans fight the Taliban."

"That's quite admirable." The woman fanned herself briefly, and then lowered her hand. "So, what brings you to our little town?"

"My friend invited me to stay with him and his sister." He spied Ryan crossing the parking lot and breathed a sigh of relief. He wasn't sure how much more of this uncomfortable wait he could endure.

Before the woman with the dog could speak again, Ryan stepped inside. He scanned the waiting room and walked over to Basir. "Vet finished?"

"Yes." Basir fought against the sadness at the recent memory of seeing the kitten breathe its last. "He says this one should be fine with plenty of formula."

The receptionist called them over, and Ryan paid the bill. Then, they left the office with the two women staring after Basir. He didn't mind leaving them behind, especially the one with the dog. Despite living with Meghan and Ryan for nearly a month, the people in this small town still couldn't seem to accept that he was a man starting a new life for himself in a safer place.

When they arrived back at the farm, Ryan gave Basir the bag containing the bottle and can of formula and went to deal with the deceased kittens. Basir took his tiny charge into the house and headed straight for the kitchen. The kitten had started acting hungry again, and Basir intended to feed the little guy any time he asked, even if it was more than every two hours.

He found a hand towel and wrapped it around the

kitten. Then he laid the small bundle on the table and turned his attention to the feeding supplies. The instructions for mixing the powdered kitten formula were simple enough, but when he looked at the bottle's packaging, he discovered a small problem. The nipple didn't have a hole in it, so the kitten wouldn't be able to eat from it.

As he searched through the drawers and found only items that would make too big a hole, the back door opened. He looked over expecting to see Ryan, but he found Meghan staring at him instead.

"What on earth is going on in here?" she asked over the plaintive mewing coming from the hand towel on the table.

Basir slowly closed the drawer of miscellaneous stuff he had been rummaging through and turned to face her. His heart pounded, and he prayed he hadn't offended her in some way. She didn't look thrilled, but on the other hand, she didn't look angry either. He opened his mouth to offer an explanation, but she rushed to the table and lifted the edge of the towel.

"Oh, the poor little thing!" She met Basir's gaze, and he found it impossible to look away as she spoke again. "Where did it come from? Where is its mother?"

"Someone hid it in a box in the weeds by the road." Basir retrieved the small bottle from the counter, hoping Meghan could help solve the feeding issue. "He needs to eat, but I can't find anything to poke a hole with. Do you have a needle or something small like that I can use?"

"I have needles in my workshop." She approached and held out her hand. "Why don't you give me the bottle? You can comfort the poor noisy baby while I make it useable."

He handed over the bottle, and she swept out of the room. Another round of mewing, accompanied by lots of squirming drew him to the towel-wrapped bundle on the table. He gently scooped it up and uncovered the kitten. It seemed oblivious to his presence until he turned it on its back and started lightly stroking its belly. The kitten stared up at him with big, blue eyes and quieted.

Meghan returned and moved to the counter where the can of formula sat. "You keep doing whatever it is that's soothing the little guy, and I'll mix up its dinner."

He watched her move with ease as she prepared the bottle, and he wondered again why no one had married her yet. Did no one notice what a wonderful woman she was? Could no one see her compassionate nature and the love that flowed from her to everyone she met?

The kitten squirmed and started complaining again, bringing his attention back to it. His musings about his best friend's sister would have to wait. Right now, the innocent life in his hands took precedence.

~*~

Meghan watched Basir coax the young, orphaned kitten into accepting the bottle, and her heart melted. Seeing a guy with a tough exterior caring for such a tiny creature was sweet enough, but the way he murmured softly to the kitten as he fed it was heartwarming. The kitten put its little front paws on the bottle and tried to knead like it would its mother, but the paws kept slipping. Basir adjusted his hold on the bottle, placing his finger where the kitten could easily reach. The poor baby put its paws on him and kneaded his skin, appearing to relax now that it had contact with something soft and warm.

Basir glanced up, his tawny eyes shining. "This little one will be fine. He is accepting the bottle with no problem, so he will soon gain the weight he is missing."

"That's a relief." Meghan watched the kitten eat a moment longer. A bit of formula seeped out of the corners of its mouth. "He's so scrawny."

"He just needs plenty to eat about every two hours." He stroked the kitten's belly with his thumb. "He will have to stay with me at night."

"That's fine. I have a couple of old towels you can use to make him a soft nest that can be easily washed in case of accidents."

Basir looked at her again. "You do not mind me keeping a cat in the house?"

"Of course not. I had a pet cat growing up. A big orange tabby named Bounce. I've just been too busy with the alpacas and my yarn business to think about getting another one."

His gaze drifted back to the kitten. "Kashmala..."

Meghan caught her breath. After what Ryan had told her about Afghan men not talking about the women in their family, she was honored and stunned that Basir was bringing up his dead wife for the second time in the short time she'd known him. She waited for what felt like an eternity before he spoke again.

"She did not approve of animals in the house," he said, his voice soft and low. "Not even a cat."

Meghan slid into the chair across from him, eager to see how long this conversation would last. "I've met a few people who feel the same way. I don't understand the reluctance to have pets, but to each his—or her—own, I guess."

Basir nodded, his gaze never leaving the creature in his hands. "You are much different than my wife was."

Disconcerted by the statement, Meghan waited a moment to see if he would clarify it. When he remained silent, she decided to take a risk. "Is that a good thing or a bad thing?"

His expression turned pensive, leaving her to wonder if she'd made a mistake by asking. But then he lifted his gaze to meet hers, and she saw the vulnerability in his eyes.

"It is a good thing. I don't think Kashmala liked me very much."

"I'm sorry to hear that." Not only had he lost his wife so young, it hadn't even been a happy marriage? She wanted to reach out and lay a hand on his arm in comfort, but she wasn't sure he was ready for that yet. He had been gradually talking to her more and with greater ease, but she knew he still had a long way to go before he could fully accept her touchy-feely American ways.

Basir shrugged as he pulled the bottle from the sleeping kitten's mouth and set it on the table. "Our families thought we would be a good match. We were not, but I cared for her."

"I'm sure you both did the best you could under the circumstances."

"I tried, anyway." He drew in a deep breath and released it on a sigh. "Meghan, I am not a good man in Afghanistan."

She struggled to get past her shock at the confession. How could such a kind and wonderful person think he wasn't a good man in his homeland? Had he changed who he was in the time since coming to the United States? She doubted it, since her brother had nothing but good things to say about Basir.

"What do you mean you're not a good man? You seem like a good man to me, and Ryan has been saying you are all along."

"To Americans I am, but to my family and my village..." He shook his head and sighed. "My honor has been destroyed there. I cannot redeem it fully, especially now that I live here. I am nothing...an outcast."

Her heart went out to him as she saw how difficult it was for him to tell her this. She wasn't even sure why he was telling her, but it made her feel special to know he trusted her enough to share something so painful.

"Basir, I know you hold onto the past and the culture you came from, but you can't let it hold you back from your future here." She took a risk and reached across the table to touch his hand. "You are an honorable man now, one I am proud to call my friend. I know Ryan feels the same way."

To her surprise, he turned his hand over and grasped her fingers. A hint of a smile lifted the corners of his mouth as he met her gaze. "It heals me to hear you say that. It gives me hope."

Before she could ask about his hopes, Ryan came in the back door. His gaze landed on their clasped hands, but he didn't immediately say anything. Instead, he went to the sink and washed his hands. Only after he'd tossed the hand towel back on the counter did he speak.

"What's going on?" He indicated their hands, and Basir released Meghan's fingers.

"Forgive me, Ryan." Basir ducked his head, appearing much guiltier than the situation called for.

Meghan met her brother's scrutiny head on. "We were talking."

Ryan nodded, his gaze going back to his friend. "Basir, I think we need to talk."

Ire rose in Meghan, lifting her to her feet. "Ryan, I don't see any reason why you need to talk to him about anything right at the moment. We were talking. That's it."

"He was holding your hand." Ryan shook his head and sighed. "I don't know how I missed it for so long."

"Missed what?"

Basir lifted his head, regret shining in his eyes. "I am attracted to you, Meghan. Forgive me for offending your family. That was not my intention."

She walked around the table and knelt beside him, ignoring her brother's irritated expression. "There's nothing to forgive. I've suspected for quite some time that you were attracted to me."

"You have?"

"Yes. I am not as blind as my brother." She laid her hand on his arm, no longer afraid to touch him. "Just so you know, the feeling is mutual."

"What?" Ryan took a step toward them.

Meghan stood and faced her brother. "Get over it. We're all adults here, and you know nothing even remotely immoral has happened. It won't either."

"That's not my problem."

"Then what is?"

Basir rose from his seat and cradled the kitten to his chest. "I am not worthy of you."

"That's not my problem, either," Ryan said.

"So, what *is* your problem?" Meghan crossed her

arms and raised her eyebrows.

"You're my sister, and he's my best friend. The thought of you guys together...just, no."

She rolled her eyes and blew out an exasperated breath. "Grow up, Ryan. We're not in middle school anymore."

"I know that!" He released a breath and headed for the hall. "I'm going out for a while."

"Will you be here for dinner?" Meghan asked, following him as far as the kitchen doorway.

"No. I'll be home sometime tonight, but don't wait up for me."

"Ryan, wait." Basir handed Meghan the kitten and followed him out the front door.

Meghan stared after them, wondering if her brother had taken complete leave of his senses. He'd been the one to encourage her to befriend Basir. Before that, he'd practically begged her to let the man stay with them, all the while insisting she would like him. And now that she and Basir admitted to their attraction for each other, Ryan threw the grown-up version of a temper tantrum?

She shook her head and stroked the silky fur of the kitten in her hands. "I sure hope you're a girl. Males make no sense."

9

"Ryan, wait!" Basir jogged to where his friend was opening his car door. "We need to talk."

"There's nothing to talk about." Ryan leaned against the door and sighed. "You and my sister like each other. I get that."

"I'm sorry." Basir briefly closed his eyes, wishing he could go back in time and tell Ryan of his attraction long ago. "I never meant to become attracted to her. I fought it as long as I could. Forgive me for giving in rather than leaving as I should have done."

"Wait. Why do you think you should have left?"

"Because I am not worthy of Meghan. By staying here and letting my attraction to her grow, I have harmed our friendship and your relationship with your sister."

"No, you haven't. Meghan and I fought all the time when we were younger, and we still argue sometimes now." Ryan reached out and laid a hand on Basir's shoulder. "My friendship with you hasn't been harmed, either. I just need time to think and to adjust to what you guys have apparently realized for weeks."

"I should still leave." Basir sighed and shook his head. "Meghan deserves a man better than me."

"Hold on. Where are you getting the idea that you're not worthy of her?"

"Look at me." Basir spread his arms and then let them fall back to his sides. "I am scarred. I have permanent brain damage. My counselor tells me I have PTSD. I have to take antidepressants and anti-anxiety medication to function. On top of that, my honor was ruined long ago, my family disowned me, and I have nothing to offer your sister. I'm not worthy of any woman, let alone one as amazing as Meghan."

"The scars, the brain damage, the PTSD, the medication...none of that stuff matters. Not to Meghan and not to me. I have enough of my own problems that I can't possibly hold yours against you." Ryan sucked in a breath and sighed. "As for your honor, you redeemed that through your work with us and through your good character. You are an honorable man. Maybe not by your village's or your family's standards, but they chose to toss you aside. Their opinions no longer count. To everyone who does count, your honor is intact and strong."

Basir longed to believe his friend's words, but he couldn't do more than hope they were true. His counselor had told him that in time, he would overcome his negative self-image, but he had a long way to go. There was one concern Ryan hadn't addressed, however. "I still have nothing to offer. Only myself, and that is broken."

"You're not broken. You're changed." Ryan straightened and combed his fingers through his hair. "Listen, I really need to get away and think. Before I go, I want you to promise me one thing...well, two things."

"What?"

"One, promise me you won't do anything stupid while I'm gone, like leave."

"I promise." Although he wasn't sure staying was the right choice, he didn't have anywhere else to go.

"What is the second thing?"

"Treat my sister right. You are the first guy since high school she's had a real interest in. That means a lot." Ryan looked him straight in the eye, and Basir saw the marine he had worked with rather than the civilian he had been living with. "Don't break her heart. If you do, you won't want to deal with me."

"I will do my best, but you know that matters of the heart are far from predictable."

"I know." Ryan looked away for a moment. When he met Basir's gaze again, the civilian man had returned. "I guess what I should say is promise me you won't intentionally hurt her."

"I would never intentionally do anything to hurt her. She is far too special and important."

"You and I agree on that one." Ryan moved to climb into his car. "I'm going to head out. See you later."

Basir watched him go down the driveway and then turn in the opposite direction of town. Sighing, he looked up at the house, but he couldn't bring himself to go inside. He couldn't face Meghan yet, not after everything he'd told her. True, she'd seemed sympathetic and afterward admitted being attracted to him, but he couldn't shake the fear that he had made a huge mistake. What had he been thinking, opening up to her? He kept those things hidden for a reason.

The lawnmower sitting in the middle of the yard caught his eye. After finding the kittens, he hadn't finished his chore. He headed for the machine, determined to finish it now. At the very least, it gave him a good reason to have some solitude so he could figure out what to do now that his feelings were out in the open.

~*~

The sound of the lawnmower shattered the quiet as Meghan settled the napping kitten in a towel-lined box. She set the box on the floor by the wall and left the kitchen, heading for the front door. A quick peek out the window beside it showed Basir pushing the mower through the grass and her brother's car missing. Well, at least her lawn wouldn't remain half-mowed for long. If only she knew Ryan would accept a relationship between her and Basir, then she could relax. For now, she had yarn waiting to be wound into skeins and packaged for sale.

Two hours later, she set the last skein into the nearly full plastic storage box and snapped the lid in place. Plaintive mewing drifted to her ears from the direction of the kitchen. She followed the sound and found the kitten wobbling around its towel-lined nest, calling as loudly as its little voice allowed.

"I hear you, babe," Meghan said as she knelt beside the box. "Are you hungry again?"

She stroked its soft fur, which quieted the cries only briefly.

"All right, little one. I'll mix up some formula for you."

She had just settled into a chair and stuck the bottle in the kitten's mouth when Basir came in. Sweat darkened his T-shirt and grass clippings clung to his sneakers and jeans. He paused and then moved to the sink.

"Thank you for feeding him. I came in to see if he was hungry."

"Yeah, he started complaining about the same

time I finished winding yarn." Suddenly, the kitten started squirming and spit out the bottle. As its cries renewed, Meghan tried without luck to feed it. "Come on, little one. You won't stop being hungry if you don't eat."

No amount of coaxing could get the nipple back in the kitten's mouth. Basir dried his hands and approached.

"Let me try." He accepted the kitten and gently stroked its body as he spoke softly. "You need to eat to feel better."

He held to bottle to its mouth, and it latched on. Sucking loudly, the kitten kneaded Basir's fingers and settled into his hand as though it belonged there. Meghan smiled and met Basir's gaze.

"I think he's definitely your baby."

Basir looked away and seated himself in a chair. His features had the same tension she'd seen far too often, especially before he said anything about his life in Afghanistan. But underneath the tension lay an intense sadness that made her want to cry without even knowing what caused it. How could pointing out that the kitten preferred him to her make him that sad?

Despite longing to ask about it, she held her tongue. Experience had shown that he would talk to her when he was ready, if he wanted her to know what was on his mind. Even though she wanted to know everything about him and his life before coming to America, she had already accepted that would likely never happen. After all, how much didn't she know about her brother's time in the marines? And she was related to him. Basir had been a stranger just a few weeks ago. Even with his increased conversational abilities, she still knew remarkably little about him.

Finally, he stroked the kitten's belly with his thumb and spoke barely above a whisper. "I almost had a baby once."

Meghan instantly regretted her choice of words when referring to the kitten. "What happened?"

"Kashmala was killed before it was born." He looked at her with damp eyes. "Even your brother doesn't know that. At the time, I couldn't tell anyone that I had been unable to protect my unborn child. It made me not only a terrible husband but a terrible father. I couldn't face that shame along with everything else."

"I'm so sorry, Basir." Tears stung her eyes at his tangible pain. How horrible must it be to carry around such a secret, to never be offered comfort for the loss of the child he had never had a chance to meet? "I hope you know that I don't think you are a terrible husband or a terrible father."

"I do." He sighed and focused on the kitten again. "It is difficult for me to feel I am a good man, especially with all that happened because I worked with the marines. But knowing you accept me and see me as good helps."

She laid her hand on his arm, feeling anything she said would be inadequate. He looked at her fingers resting on his warm skin, and then he lifted his gaze to hers.

"We have not talked about my attraction to you." He cleared his throat. "I have nothing to offer you but the broken man you see."

"I don't see a broken man." She gave his arm a gentle squeeze and withdrew her hand. "I see a man who has suffered a great deal. A man who is trying to find his way in a new land with a new way of life. I see a man I would like to get to know better and spend more time with."

"Ryan agrees with you that I am not broken. He says I am changed." He shook his head. "But I feel broken, even if you don't see me that way."

"Broken things can be repaired and made whole again. There will be scars, but those are evidence of healed wounds."

"Like my eyes," he said softly.

"Exactly like that." She wanted to touch the scar tissue just to show him it didn't bother her, but she sensed that would be too intimate in his mind. "I want to help you heal if I can. If you'll let me. But you're going to have to tell me what would help you. I don't know what to do on my own."

"Be you. The way you accept me for who I am now and treat me with kindness no matter what I reveal to you...that is beginning to heal the broken places inside me. I still have much healing to do, but like I said earlier, you give me hope."

The sincerity in his voice filled her heart to overflowing. She could easily continue to treat him the same way she had been, nurturing the friendship she hoped would continue to strengthen and grow. A romantic relationship might take some time and creativity to develop, but she had a feeling his openness with her was his way of developing that relationship. Perhaps she could help him experience the American way of romance. A quick glance at the clock revealed it was nearing dinner time, and she decided to take full advantage of their need to eat.

"I hope you don't mind if I change the subject, but what do you think of having pizza for dinner?"

"Pizza is good."

"In that case, why don't you put the kitten in its nest over there?" She indicated the box against the wall with a wave of her hand. "We can go into town to the best pizza place around."

"Meghan..." His internal struggle showed in his face and eyes. "I can't."

"Why not?" She thought she knew the answer, but she needed to hear it from him.

"I am Afghan. Sitting here with you, alone...it is difficult, but I will do it because I enjoy your company and I know that this is how it is done in America. But going out with you alone, in public, is too much right now. I want to be able to take you on a date someday, but this is all still too new for me." Basir shrugged, looking so uncertain that she wanted to smack herself for pushing him. "Do you mind too much if we don't go into town tonight?"

"It's fine. I can order the pizza and have it delivered." She bit her lip and fought the urge to cry. "Will you forgive me for pushing too hard? I'm still trying to learn and adjust to a different way of doing things too, and I don't always know when to back off."

"There is nothing to forgive." A faint smile lifted the corners of his mouth. "There are times I need to be pushed to let go of the old ways and live by the new."

He set the empty bottle on the table and rose from his seat. After settling the kitten in its towel-lined box, he turned to Meghan once more.

"I will go clean up now."

He left the room without another word, and she stared after him long after he disappeared up the stairs. Despite her joy at Basir finally talking to her about himself and his past, she was overwhelmed. His new openness felt as though their relationship had progressed from barely friends to something intensely intimate in a matter of minutes. That he'd admitted the loss of his unborn child, a fact he hadn't even told Ryan, was huge. She couldn't help feeling as if he was already thinking of marriage while she was still considering the first date.

Not for the first time, she wished she could seek her twin's wisdom and advice concerning romance in Afghanistan. But after his overreaction to learning of Basir's attraction to her and vice versa, she didn't dare ask him how it all worked. No, she would have to figure it out on her own with only her Heavenly Father to guide her.

10

The sound of a vehicle coming down the long drive shattered the late-night silence. Basir tensed as memories from his homeland flooded his mind, but then reason kicked in. The vehicle was probably Ryan's car. Still, as the only man currently in the house, he was responsible for Meghan's safety.

With that thought in mind, he left his bed, taking care not to disturb the kitten slumbering in the box beside it. As he headed downstairs, he heard the front door open and close. Despite his certainty that it was just Ryan arriving home, every fiber of his being prepared to defend Meghan with his life, if necessary.

He reached the first floor at the same time Ryan stepped into view. His friend's eyes widened and his step faltered, but then he relaxed and smiled.

"Hey, man. I didn't expect anyone to still be awake."

"I heard your car on the driveway and wanted to make sure it really was you." Basir studied him but saw no sign of his earlier anger. "I felt it was my responsibility to protect your sister in your absence."

"I'm glad to know you're looking out for her." Ryan shifted his weight and sighed. "I'm sorry for the way I left earlier, but you guys shocked me."

"Forgive me." Basir placed his hand over his heart.

"There's nothing to forgive." Ryan glanced up the stairs and met Basir's gaze. "Let's go to the kitchen to

E. A. West

talk. I don't want to disturb Meghan."

Once they were seated at the kitchen table, Ryan spoke again.

"I've had plenty of time to think about you guys liking each other, and I still don't know how I missed it for so long. Thinking back, I should have seen the signs weeks ago. Out of curiosity, just how long have you been interested in my sister?"

Basir dreaded answering, but he couldn't lie to the man. "Do you remember the photograph you showed me while we were still in Afghanistan? The one of Meghan with her hair loose?"

Ryan's eyebrows headed for his hairline. "You've liked her that long?"

"She is a beautiful woman." He shrugged, hoping his friend wouldn't be offended by the blunt statement. "When you showed me her picture, I only wished I would have the chance to meet her someday. Then, when you brought me here and I did meet her...I think that is when the attraction truly started."

"I see." Ryan looked away, his expression impossible to decipher. "I want you to know I think the two of you are perfect for each other. My problem earlier was all me. It wasn't anything you or Meghan said or did."

"Will you tell me what the problem was?"

"My two worlds collided, and I wasn't prepared for it." The intensity in Ryan's haunted gaze was unsettling. "I've always tried to shield Meghan from knowing what my life was really like during my deployments. You were a part of those deployments, so you know everything. The two of you getting together is like having two different parts of me getting together, and it's hard. Don't get me wrong. I'm happy

126

for you guys. I just need to figure out how to handle having my life as a marine becoming a part of my life as Meghan's brother."

Basir leaned forward. "You know I will do everything I can to take care of Meghan and protect her."

"I know, and that's one of the reasons I approve of you for her. You're a good man, and you'll treat her right." Ryan shook his head and leaned back. "It's like I said, this is my problem alone and really doesn't have a lot to do with you guys. It's just the weird stuff going on in my head that's causing the issue. I plan to talk to my counselor about it the next time I see him."

"I am not the only who needs help adjusting to a new way of life?" Basir smiled, enjoying evidence that someone else struggled with changes.

Ryan chuckled. "No, I need help with that too from time to time. Speaking of a new way of life...I know casual dating is a no-go where you come from. Have you decided to give it a shot now that you're integrating into American society, or do you have something more permanent in mind for my sister?"

Heat infused Basir from head to toe. How could he admit to the depth of his feelings so soon after admitting he had the feelings in the first place? "I would like to get to know Meghan and develop a relationship with her."

Ryan scrutinized him and leaned forward. "What kind of relationship?"

"Whatever kind she is willing to have with me."

"Marriage?"

"Perhaps someday, if she is willing." Basir wished Ryan didn't know him and Afghan culture so well.

"Does she know how strongly you feel?"

"I don't know. I haven't told her yet. It is too soon for that."

"Are you sure?"

"No. I am still learning about romantic relationships in America. If we were in Afghanistan, I would have my father talk to your father."

"That's pretty serious." Ryan studied him a moment longer. "If at some point you decide you want to talk to our father about a future with Meghan, I'll give you his phone number. But you'll need to talk to Meghan first. We don't do arranged marriages in my family."

An arranged marriage would make things so much easier, but he understood that wouldn't work. Thoughts of possible marriage at some point in the future brought out his doubts full force. "I don't know if I am worthy of marrying your sister yet. There is still much from my past that must be laid to rest."

Ryan heaved a sigh. "I'm too tired to argue with you again about your worthiness. Let's both go get some sleep, and maybe by morning you'll realize you're worth as much as the rest of us, regardless of what happened in the past."

They rose from their seats, but Basir stopped Ryan before they left the kitchen. "You will not tell Meghan how I strongly feel for her?"

"Nope. That's up to you to tell her." Ryan grinned and clapped a hand to his shoulder. "I may be her brother and your friend, but you guys are on your own for making this romance work."

He headed into the hall, and Basir stared after him. Romance? Somewhere inside, he knew that's precisely what it was, but hearing the word out loud was still intimidating. He knew nothing about romancing a woman. That could have been part of why Kashmala hadn't liked him. He had tried to woo her after their wedding, but his attempts had been awkward at best.

"Father God, please grant me the wisdom to do this properly," he whispered. "You know how I feel about Meghan and my hopes for the future. Please help me to let go of the past so I can move forward."

Even though he didn't suddenly gain any insight into how to handle the situation or have any instantaneous healing from all he had suffered, he felt better knowing the situation lay firmly in God's hands. He headed for the stairs and hoped the next day would bring him the confidence he needed to build an American-style relationship.

~*~

Meghan didn't see her brother until the middle of the morning. He walked into her workshop and dropped onto the bench by the wall as she boxed up a small order of yarn. She waited for him to speak, but he was still silent when she attached the label to the box and set it aside to take to the post office later.

She braced her hands on the table and studied him. "Are you over whatever was going on with you last night?"

"No, but that's going to take a while to get over." He looked away, and she was struck by how similar the gesture was to Basir.

"Come on, Ryan." She blew out an exasperated breath and crossed her arms. "You knew I would fall for someone at some point, and I happen to know you like Basir. Why can't you be happy he's the one I'm interested in?"

E. A. West

"I am happy about that." He met her gaze, and she couldn't deny the sincerity she saw there. "Like I told him when I got home last night, I think you guys are perfect for each other."

"So, why are you acting like the thought of us dating is torturing you?"

"Because it kind of is." He rose and paced across the room. "Like I explained to Basir, I've worked so hard to keep my time in Afghanistan separate from my life here. I wanted to leave that time in the past where it belongs."

"Then why did you want to bring Basir here in the first place?" She was suddenly glad the man in question was out doing something with the alpacas. With the way this conversation was going, poor Basir would likely assume it was against him somehow.

"He needed a place to stay, and I owed him a lot." Ryan faced her again. "I knew it was a risk bringing him here, but I never expected the two of you to fall for each other. Now that you have...it's like having both parts of my life slam together with no warning. I can't pretend to keep them separate any longer. I know you can't possibly understand that, but it's unbelievably difficult for me right now."

"I'm sorry, Ryan." She walked over and gave him a hug. "Is there anything I can do to make the adjustment easier for you?"

He chuckled and stepped back. "It's not as easy as changing the clothes you wear this time."

Her face burned, and she ducked her head. "Basir told you about that?"

"Yes, but I'd pretty much figured it out on my own. After all, it was kind of obvious you suddenly stopped wearing shorts and tank tops."

"Oh." She should have realized that, but with as oblivious as he'd been to Basir liking her, she'd assumed he hadn't notice the difference in her clothing choices either.

"That's one of the reasons I think you and Basir are perfect for each other. Not many women would change what they wear on the off chance it would allow them to befriend a guy who's painfully shy around them."

"You know I like to help people if I can."

"I do, but there's really nothing you can do to help me adjust." He held up his hand when she opened her mouth to protest. "It's something I have to deal with myself, in my own way. I've already set up an appointment with my counselor to help me work through it all."

"OK." The sense of helplessness frustrated her, especially since she knew her attraction to his friend was responsible for his current distress. "You'll let me know if there's anything I can do?"

"Of course." He hugged her and stepped back with a smile. "You're a good woman, Megs. Basir's lucky to have you."

She sighed. "I keep hoping he'll realize something similar to that, but it's hard to know what he's feeling."

"You don't have anything to worry about. He likes you, and he's made it clear in his own way." Ryan tugged her ponytail. "You just don't understand romance in Afghanistan."

"That's because I've never been there, unlike some people I know." She crossed her arms and raised her eyebrows, relieved to see her brother in a better mood. "I don't suppose you'd care to give me a few pointers?"

"Keep doing whatever you've been doing. It seems to be working out pretty well."

"You're no help."

"Of course not. I already told Basir you guys are on your own for figuring this out. I'm not about to let you turn me into a hypocrite."

Meghan rolled her eyes. "I should get Julia to find you a date just so I can refuse to give you any pointers."

"I don't need any." Ryan headed for the door but paused and glanced over his shoulder. "I don't need Julia's help to find a date either."

Meghan stared after him as he left the room. That last comment sounded suspiciously like he had a girlfriend hidden somewhere or maybe just someone he was interested in. Her joking comment about finding a date sprang to mind and touched off an idea.

Basir wasn't comfortable going on a date with her without a chaperone nearby. If Ryan already had a woman he was dating, maybe she could talk both guys into a double date. Not only would it give her the opportunity to go out with Basir, but she would also get a chance to satisfy her curiosity about her brother's love life.

She smiled as she turned to pick up the box waiting to be shipped. "Thank You, Lord, for giving me a creative mind."

11

Basir tossed another handful of green beans into the five-gallon bucket and looked across the garden. Ryan picked tomatoes off to the left, while Meghan plucked cucumbers from vines on the right. He glanced at the sun sinking toward the horizon. They only had an hour or two of daylight left. Thankfully, they were almost finished with harvesting. A dull headache had dogged him all afternoon, but he was grateful it hadn't progressed to worse pain.

He picked the green beans from the last bush and lifted the mostly full bucket. After dropping it off by the trailer Ryan had hooked to Meghan's truck earlier that afternoon, he stopped by the upside-down laundry basket resting in the shade of a tree. He removed the rock from the top and lifted the basket, revealing the month-old kitten playing beneath it.

"Hello, little one," he said as he stroked the kitten's body. Regular, round-the-clock feedings had given it a healthy weight and even softer fur. "Having fun?"

The kitten pounced on his hand and gave his fingers a gentle bite. Basir chuckled and pulled his hand away.

"I will take that as a yes." He stroked the kitten one last time, and then replaced the basket and the rock.

He didn't like keeping the little creature contained

in such a way, but he still needed to keep the kitten close by for ease of feeding. In another week he would be able to leave him alone for longer periods of time. Already the kitten ate less frequently than he had at the beginning, but Basir still wasn't comfortable leaving him alone in the house long enough to harvest.

Ignoring the kitten's mew of complaint, he returned to the garden. Ryan carried a box of tomatoes toward the trailer, but Meghan was still picking. Basir joined her and moved to the other side of the string trellis covered with vines. As he picked a ripe cucumber, he heard Meghan stop.

"You don't have to help," she said. "I know you've been struggling with a headache this afternoon."

"It is not too bad." He picked another cucumber and handed both vegetables to her. "Besides, you have been out here longer than I have."

"True, but I'm used to it. I've been selling at the farmer's market since my second summer on the farm."

He shook his head and smiled. "You are a stubborn woman, Meghan. Let me help you finish. There's not much more."

"If you want to pick cucumbers that badly, who am I to complain?" She set the vegetables in the box by her feet and moved down the row.

Ten minutes later, they met at the end of the trellis. Meghan took the last cucumbers from Basir, and her smile brightened the fading sunlight.

"Thanks, Basir. I appreciate the help."

"You're welcome." He wanted to say more, something witty like he'd seen other men do when talking to beautiful women, but not a single thing came to mind. The full box sitting on the ground caught his attention. If he couldn't impress her with his words, maybe he could impress her with his work ethic. "I will take this to the trailer for you."

"All right." She set the cucumbers she held in the box and stepped back. "Thank you."

Basir lifted the heavy box and carried it away, feeling her gaze burning into his back. Ahead of him, Ryan stood by the trailer watching his approach. While it was nice to have a chaperone and the knowledge that Ryan approved of him for Meghan, Basir couldn't shake the negative little voice in the back of his mind. It constantly listed all the reasons why a relationship with Meghan was a bad idea and reminded him of why he wasn't worthy of any woman. His counselor had given him some ideas to help quiet that voice, but all he'd managed to do so far was muffle it a little. It didn't help that the negative thoughts about himself were in his father's and grandfather's voices. Both men had been against him working with the Americans, but he had followed his heart. After his wife's murder, they had said terrible things to him and about him before disowning him in an attempt to keep themselves and the rest of the family from meeting the same fate as Kashmala.

He had worked so hard to move past all of that, but it seemed that no matter what he did, those memories wouldn't let him go. Thinking about his hope of a future with Meghan, he couldn't help worrying what her parents would think of him. Yes, he had Ryan's support and approval, but would that be enough to gain their father's blessing?

Ryan took the box of cucumbers from Basir's arms and set it with the rest of the harvest. "Surely you don't find it that distasteful to talk to my sister."

"What?" Basir studied him, uncertain of why he would say such a thing.

"You talked to Meghan for a minute, and now you look like you want to crawl in a hole and die. Since she looks pretty happy, I'm guessing she didn't say anything terrible to you."

"No, it is nothing she said." He sighed and looked toward the alpaca pasture on the far side of the barn. "My past still haunts me and attempts to drown my hope for the future."

"You're going to have to let go of that stuff, or it's never going to work between you and Meghan."

"I know, and I am trying to let it go. But *you* know that it is not so easy to move past anything that happened in Afghanistan."

"Yes, I do. I'm still trying to move past what I went through, and you have a lot more than I do." Ryan shook his head and blew out a breath. "I just don't want to see you or Meghan get hurt because of what happened in the past."

"I will do my best to protect her." Basir debated how much he should say, and then he decided to be completely honest for his friend's peace of mind. "I have talked to her about some of the things in my past. It is difficult, but it has helped us become better friends."

"I'm glad to hear it." Ryan opened his mouth as if to say more, but he closed it again as Meghan joined them.

"Hey, I have a great idea," she said with a smile.

"What's that?" Ryan asked.

"You guys can come up with something for dinner while I cut the herbs and store them in the fridge."

"I have an even better idea." Ryan grinned at

Basir, and then focused on his sister. "I'll run into town and pick up some food, and Basir can stay here and help you out."

"That is a better idea." Meghan's face lit up and set Basir's heart racing. After Ryan climbed in his car, she turned to Basir. "I am so happy right now."

"Because I am going to help you cut the herbs?"

Her light laugh floated on the breeze. "That too, but mostly because Ryan is definitely willing to accept a relationship between us."

"He told me the night he found out we like each other that he thinks we are perfect for each other." Had he not talked to his sister and assured he wasn't angry?

"He told me the same thing the next morning, but actions speak a lot louder than words. This proves he meant what he said."

"Good point." Basir lifted a hand toward the beds of herbs. "Shall we get to work so we can finish before it is dark?"

As they started harvesting a variety of herbs, Basir felt a spark ignite in his soul. Perhaps a future with Meghan wasn't such a bad idea after all. Now that Ryan was blatantly encouraging them to spend time alone together, Basir could believe he would also support their relationship if his parents turned out to be against it. And Meghan's joy at her brother's support gave him confidence that she truly did want a relationship with him—scars, bad memories, and all.

~*~

Meghan adjusted the display of yarn at the end of one table, pleased with how quickly the booth had come together. With both Ryan and Basir assisting her with the set up, it had gone much faster than usual. All they had left to do now was relax until the farmer's market opened and the customers arrived.

"Sorry, little one, you have to share the chair with me," Basir said behind her, a touch of amusement in his voice.

She turned around to find him lifting his kitten from the seat of a camp chair. He had fashioned a harness and leash for it with some twine he had found in the barn, and the kitten had quickly adjusted to wearing it. Now he just seemed happy to have his human cuddling him.

"You know," she said as she walked closer, "that little guy really needs a name. You've had him a little over a week already, so I think it's pretty safe to assume he's a permanent member of your family."

Basir looked up at her and stroked the month-old kitten's side. "He has a name."

"Really? What is it?" She'd never heard him call the kitten by anything resembling a name.

"Kadwaal."

A burst of laughter came from Ryan at the front of the booth. "Seriously? That's what you named him?"

Basir smiled and nodded. "I thought it appropriate."

Meghan shifted her gaze between the two men, feeling a little left out. "What does the name mean?"

"It means refugee," Basir said and petted the kitten trying to suck on his finger. "Kadwaal was forced from his home, so in a way he is a refugee."

"You're right. It is appropriate." She turned to her brother and lifted her eyebrows. "Just how much Pashto do you know?"

"Not as much as Basir, but enough to recognize

some words and phrases." Ryan sprawled in another camp chair. "He's a good teacher, and we had plenty of time to talk."

Meghan sat in the third chair, on the other side of Basir, and studied her brother. "I'm beginning to think I don't really know you anymore."

"You still know me, Megs." Ryan leaned forward and braced his forearms on his knees. "Yeah, there's a lot you don't know, but I'm still your brother."

"True. I think it's just soaking in that you and I haven't shared everything about our lives in years." She relaxed against the back of her chair and sighed, aware of Basir listening closely. "I kind of miss being that close to you."

"We grew up to be different people with vastly different lives." Ryan shrugged when she glanced at him. "If it helps, you know a lot about my life now."

"Except for who you're dating."

"Who says I'm dating anyone?"

"You told me you didn't need Julia to find you a date. Doesn't that mean you've already found your own?"

"Maybe." Ryan stood and stretched. "I'm going to walk around for a bit."

"Are you going to tell me who she is before you go?"

"Nope." He grinned, winked, and then walked away.

Meghan stared after him, trying to understand why her brother was still as exasperating now as he had been when they were kids.

"Her name is Sara," Basir said.

"What?" She turned toward him.

"The woman Ryan is interested in. Her name is

Sara."

"How do you know that?"

"He told me her name before I moved into your house, and he has spoken of no other woman since." Basir smiled and lifted a shoulder. "I don't know if he has taken her on a date yet, but he has talked to her on the phone several times."

"Really." She never would have guessed that Basir would know so much about her brother's love life, but it made sense. Who better to discuss a romantic interest with than your best friend?

Basir nodded and settled the kitten in his lap. "I think that sometimes when he leaves and is gone for hours, he meets her somewhere. He hasn't said anything about it, but there are times he seems unusually content when he returns."

"I've noticed that, but I never thought it was because he had a girlfriend." Meghan shook her head. "I don't know why that never occurred to me."

"Because your brother is quite good at keeping secrets." Humor twinkled in Basir's eyes. "But he forgets how good my memory is and how many things he has told me."

She laughed, almost as pleased to have inside information on her brother as she was that Basir seemed perfectly comfortable carrying on a conversation with her.

Ryan stayed gone for most of the morning, leaving Meghan and Basir to tend the customers. To Meghan's surprise, Basir was an excellent salesman and quite knowledgeable about the produce they were selling. She longed to ask him where his experience had come from, but the market was unusually busy and prevented much conversation. Shortly after Ryan brought sandwiches for lunch, things slowed down.

"You are really good at this," Meghan said, her gaze on Basir. "Where did you learn how to sell produce?"

"I grew up on a farm." He shrugged and fed Kadwaal a bite of meat from his sandwich. "As a child, I went with my father to sell our produce in the market. When I was older, I sometimes went on my own."

"I thought you came from a sheep farming family."

"My grandfather raised the sheep and taught me to care for them, but my father raised vegetables and taught me that business."

"Wow. I'm impressed." She'd had no idea how business-savvy he was, but thinking back on the time since he had started helping her with the alpacas and the garden, she could see it. He had made several suggestions to conserve resources while increasing production, and his knowledge of sheep farming had translated remarkably well to alpaca farming. For the first time since she bought her farm, she felt as though she had a partner as invested in the operation as she was. It was a strange feeling, especially since she had no idea how long he would be living and working on her farm.

"It's no big deal. Everyone where I come from knows at least a little about farming. It is how we feed our families and provide for them." Despite his attempt to downplay his abilities, the warm smile he gave her indicated how much her compliment meant to him.

"So," Ryan said, interrupting the sweet moment, "I've got a great idea for next weekend."

"Oh?" Meghan remembered some of his great ideas from the past and hoped this one wasn't like his ideas in high school.

"How would you guys like to go on your first date together?" He focused on Basir. "It would be a double date, so you'd have your chaperones."

"A double date?" Meghan said before Basir could speak. "With who?"

"Me and my date." The smirk on his face indicated he thought he knew more than she did.

She couldn't resist teasing him. "Your date? You mean Sara?"

Ryan's eyes widened. "How do you know who she is?"

"I have my ways." She grinned as Basir covered a laugh with an unconvincing cough. "So, are you going to tell me about Sara and how long you've been dating her?"

"I've only gone out with her a few times, but I met her not too long after I moved in with you." A sappy smile spread across his face, and he leaned back in his chair. "She works at the feed store, and she sells a few things now and then here at the farmer's market."

"That's why you've been so willing to go to the feed store for me. And I thought you were just trying to be nice."

"Well, that too. But, yeah, I always enjoy the chance to talk to Sara for a few minutes if she happens to be working." The sappy smile disappeared, and he straightened. "So, does that satisfy your curiosity?"

"Not even close. Were you hanging out with her all morning?"

"Only most of it. I was also talking to a guy looking to hire someone."

"You were?" Meghan's heart thumped with excitement. If he was looking for a job, that meant he was finally ready to fully participate in life again. "How did that go?"

"I have an interview Tuesday." Ryan grinned. "You might not be stuck with me much longer, Megs."

She caught Basir's sharp intake of breath, but chose to ignore it for the moment. "You don't have to leave just because you get a job. My farm is your home for however long you want it."

"I know, but I'd like to get out on my own at some point." Ryan glanced at Basir then returned his gaze to her. "Don't worry. I won't be moving for at least a couple of months. I need to save up a little before I try to find a place."

"As long as you know there's no rush." Although she was happy for her brother, she would miss having him around all the time when he moved out.

"I do." Ryan cleared his throat. "Now, you guys still haven't given me an opinion on a double date next weekend."

Meghan turned to Basir and found him looking at her. "What do you think?"

"It could be fun," he said slowly, searching her face. "Is it something you want to do?"

"Assuming Ryan doesn't have anything too crazy in mind for the date, yes."

"Since when have I suggested crazy things for dates?" Ryan asked, his tone indignant.

"Junior year of high school. We went on a double date where you had the supposedly great idea to climb a rock wall." Meghan returned her gaze to Basir. "His date turned out to be terrified of heights, and mine somehow broke a finger."

Basir chuckled and looked at Ryan. "I have to agree with your sister. No crazy ideas."

"Come on! I was barely seventeen."

"And now you are older, but are you wiser?"

"That's cold, man," Ryan said with a laugh. "You'll be relieved to know Sara and I both agreed a picnic in the park would be the perfect date."

Basir glanced at Meghan, and she nodded. He focused on Ryan once more. "A picnic sounds good. We will go on your double date."

"Great! I'll go tell Sara." Ryan rose from his seat.

"Do we get to meet her before next weekend?" Meghan asked, curiosity about her brother's girlfriend threatening to drive her nuts.

"Sure. I'll bring her by the booth later."

After Ryan left, Meghan and Basir finished their lunch between helping customers. By the end of the market, she was beginning to wonder if her brother really would bring Sara to meet them. As they packed up the small amount of remaining produce, Ryan finally showed up with a pretty brown-haired woman in her early twenties.

"This is Sara Gotheridge." He smiled at her. "Sara, that's my sister, Meghan, and my good friend, Basir Hamidi."

"It's so good to meet you," Sara said, a smile lighting her face. "Ryan tells me we're all going on a picnic next weekend."

"That's right." Meghan studied her and could see why Ryan liked her. The woman was cute and had a sweet personality that shone brightly. "You and I will have to talk about who's bringing what in the way of food. I have a feeling the guys won't be volunteering for that."

Sara laughed and hooked an arm through Ryan's. "I have the same feeling. I'll get your number from Ryan later and give you a call."

They talked a little longer, and Meghan couldn't stop a twinge of jealousy. Ryan and Sara interacted with such ease and had no problem linking arms or holding hands. She yearned for the day Basir showed such affection toward her, but she knew it could be a very long wait. With as long as it had taken him to feel comfortable talking to her for more than thirty seconds, it could be months before he held her hand in public.

Still, she wouldn't trade him for anything. He was a wonderful man, if more reserved than she was used to. And the way he looked at her, more openly now than before, melted her heart with every glance.

12

Saturday morning arrived in a burst of sunlight and singing birds. Basir barely opened his eyes before snapping them shut with a groan. Of all the days to have a migraine that made him even more light sensitive than usual, why did it have to be this one? At least the picnic was scheduled for late afternoon rather than lunch. He stood a small chance of recovering by then, but only if he managed to brave the light threatening to scorch his optic nerves and took his meds.

A soft paw stroked his face, and an equally soft mew accompanied by remarkably loud purring reminded him of a responsibility that couldn't be ignored, regardless of whether his head was going to explode.

He opened his eyes only a slit and met the innocent greenish-blue gaze of his constant companion. "Morning, Kadwaal. You are ready for breakfast, aren't you?"

The kitten purred even louder and batted his nose. Despite the spikes of pain going through his skull, Basir smiled. He never would have imagined how much an abandoned kitten could improve his outlook on life.

"All right, little one. We will get food for you and water for me."

He stifled another groan and rolled out of bed.

After donning his glasses, he scooped up the kitten and retrieved his prescription bottle from the dresser. By the time he reached the kitchen, he was ready to curl up on the floor and die. This was one of the worst headaches he'd had since he woke up in the hospital after the explosion that had done so much damage. Thankfully, he saw no sign of Meghan or Ryan. He wasn't up to pleasant chatter.

"I hope no one minds if I shirk my alpaca care responsibilities," he muttered in Pashto, too miserable to think of the English words. "I'll be lucky if I make it back to bed."

While Kadwaal played on the floor, Basir filled a glass with water and took his migraine medicine. Then he measured dry kitten food into a small bowl and mixed up enough formula to moisten it. The smell was enough to make him nauseous, or perhaps it was his headache. Either way, he knew skipping breakfast would be in his best interest.

"You get to eat upstairs," he said as he scooped up the kitten once more. He didn't have the strength or energy to stay downstairs long enough for Kadwaal to eat in the kitchen like he normally did. The sooner he went back to bed, the better.

Once in his room, he set the kitten and the bowl of softened food on the floor and fell across his bed. As he listened to Kadwaal eat, he managed to work up the motivation to take off his glasses. Crawling under the covers was beyond him. He rolled onto his side and curled up, praying for the pain and nausea to go away. With his first date with Meghan on the line, he had to get better by that afternoon. He couldn't bear to disappoint her by canceling, especially since it was a physical weakness creating the problem.

If only he had never agreed to the double date, he wouldn't have anything to worry about.

But could he really regret agreeing to move his relationship with Meghan forward a step? He cared about her deeply. If he was completely honest with himself, he might have even more affection for her than he ever had for Kashmala. He didn't know if that made him a terrible person, but right at the moment he couldn't bring himself to care. Maybe once his migraine was gone, he could give the realization the proper consideration. For now, his only goal was to recover before it was time to leave.

A slight shifting of the mattress at the foot of the bed caught his attention, and he opened his eyes far enough to see Kadwaal sitting on the corner and watching him. The brightness in the room sent another knife through Basir's skull, and he snapped his eyes shut again as he wished he would have remembered to close the curtains. Doing it now would take more effort than he could muster. At least he had managed to stack boxes just right to create a stairway for the kitten to get on and off the bed safely. Moving enough to lift the kitten was sure to kill him at the moment.

He tracked Kadwaal's movement up the bed by the light tug of the covers with each tiny step. When the kitten reached his head, it rubbed against his face and purred. The soft fur gave him something to focus on other than his misery for a brief moment, and he thanked God for providing him with a furry friend. Kadwaal would never hold the migraines against him, and already the young kitten worked to find the best way to comfort him when one hit.

As the kitten settled on his pillow, Basir prayed once more for the strength to endure the vicious headache and for his Heavenly Father's healing touch. With the way he felt, only a miracle would enable him to go on a picnic that evening.

~*~

Meghan kicked off her barn shoes and stepped sock-footed into the kitchen. The morning had passed in a blur of chores, but she couldn't shake her concern for Basir. He hadn't come down for breakfast, so Ryan volunteered to care for the alpacas. She had stayed busy in the garden, weeding and harvesting a load of cucumbers for the local grocery. Yet one eye had always been on the house, hoping to catch a glimpse of Basir.

Now it was nearly lunch time, and she still hadn't seen any sign of him. She didn't want to think he was avoiding her, but with their date later that afternoon, she couldn't keep the thought from crossing her mind. He had seemed excited about going out with her, but could he have changed his mind? True, he had been a little nervous when Ryan mentioned their date last night, but so was she. A few nerves were a natural reaction to a first date, but she wasn't going to call it off. She had waited far too long for this day. But did Basir feel the same?

"Lord, give me strength," she whispered and then sighed. Surely, he would have told her if he had changed his mind. With his extreme focus on honor, he wouldn't stand her up without a word.

Which left her with the worry that had dogged her all morning. Something must have happened to keep him from helping with the chores or even showing up for breakfast. His kitten flashed to mind, and she glanced toward its food bowl—a bowl that was conspicuously absent. OK, so maybe he had been up at some point. But why would he take the kitten's bowl somewhere else? He always fed the little guy in the kitchen while they ate breakfast.

She scanned the kitchen, searching for more clues. Her heart sank when she spotted the prescription bottle sitting beside the sink. A quick check of the label confirmed her suspicion. The poor guy had woken up with a migraine again.

After washing the accumulated grime from her hands, she grabbed the pill bottle and headed upstairs. As late as it was, if he was still suffering, she would suggest postponing the picnic. Although it would be disappointing to have to wait, she wanted him to be able to enjoy their time together too.

Basir's door was closed, and she didn't hear any sounds inside. He might be asleep, but she didn't feel right just opening the door to check. She took a deep breath to calm a sudden attack of nerves and tapped lightly on the door.

A male voice responded with something that didn't quite sound like incoherent gibberish, but it definitely wasn't English.

Uncertainty hit, and she hesitated. Maybe she shouldn't have bothered him? Too late to worry about it now. "Basir?"

Silence stretched until she was ready to scream or cry, she wasn't sure which.

"Come in." Although more heavily accented than usual, at least it was in English.

She twisted the knob and pushed open the door. Basir—sans glasses—was stretched out on his bed. He wore a T-shirt and lounge pants, similar to what her brother wore for pajamas. His kitten lay on his pillow, curled around his head.

Meghan smiled and indicated the kitten. "It looks like your furry friend is trying to make you feel better."

"Yes." He reached up and stroked his fingers along Kadwaal's small body. A purr vibrated through the air.

"Is he helping?" From where she stood just inside the room, Basir didn't appear to be in too much pain.

"Surprisingly, yes." He sighed and reached for the glasses lying on the nightstand. "Forgive me for not taking care of the alpacas this morning."

"There's nothing to forgive," she said, following her brother's example. "Ryan took care of them. When you didn't come down for breakfast, we figured you weren't up to dealing with them."

Never mind that she and Ryan had both been wrong about the cause. They had mistakenly assumed Basir overslept due to nightmares or the memories that so frequently haunted him. Why, when they both knew of his migraines, had neither of them considered that possibility? Whatever the reason, it didn't matter now.

"You left your medicine on the kitchen counter." Meghan held up the bottle. "I thought I'd bring it up to you and see how you're feeling."

"Thank you." Basir sat up and paused for a moment before standing. "I am certain I will live now."

"Was that ever in question?" She handed him the bottle when he approached.

"When I first woke up, yes." He shook his head and set his medicine on the dresser next to three other matching bottles. "I have not suffered like that in months."

"I'm glad you're feeling better now."

"So am I." He drew in a breath and released it slowly. "Where is Ryan?"

Meghan opened her mouth to reply, but the distant sound of the back door closing cut her off. She waved a hand toward the hall. "Probably wondering when I'm going to fix lunch."

Basir cracked a small smile. "You should go feed him. I know how much work the alpacas are."

"Am I feeding you too?"

"Yes. I will be down shortly."

"All right." She stepped into the hall.

Before she could close the door, Basir spoke again. "Thank you for coming to check on me. I appreciate your concern."

She turned around and smiled. "That's what people do when they care about each other."

"Yes, this is true." He looked toward the kitten still sprawled on his pillow.

Meghan waited a moment to see if he would add any more. When he remained silent, she reached for the doorknob. "See you in the kitchen."

She pulled the door closed and went downstairs. Ryan stood by the kitchen sink with a partial glass of water in his hand.

"How's Basir doing?"

"What makes you think I checked on him?" She crossed her arms and raised her eyebrows.

"I'm your brother, remember? I know you." Ryan took a drink and smirked. "So, how is he?"

She should know better than to try to hide anything from her twin. He had always been able to read her as clearly as his own thoughts. "Certain he'll live. He'll be down for lunch in a few minutes."

"Good. Did he tell you why he skipped

breakfast?"

"He woke up with a massive migraine." She moved to the refrigerator and opened it. "What do you think about sandwiches for lunch?"

"Works for me."

As she prepared sandwiches and a salad, Basir entered the kitchen with Kadwaal on his heels. He and Ryan launched a discussion of the alpacas and their care, and Meghan hoped it meant Basir had fully recovered from his headache. Since he appeared fine and wanted lunch, she could safely assume he was all right. Either that or he was a great actor, something she hadn't seen evidence of yet.

Halfway through lunch, Ryan set down his sandwich and focused on Basir. "So, are we still on for tonight, or do we need to move the picnic to another day?"

"Today is fine."

Meghan couldn't completely let go of her concern. "Are you sure? I'd rather postpone than have you unable to enjoy the evening."

"I will be fine." He offered a brief smile. "My head is much better now, and it is still improving."

She couldn't tell from his expression whether he was telling the truth or if it was a case of wishful thinking. "Well, if it gets worse or you change your mind, let me know."

"I will, but you don't need to worry. We will still have our picnic with Ryan and Sara today."

The affection and determination in his eyes did more to reassure her than his words. She had a feeling he was as intent on seeing their first date succeed as she was.

13

Basir set the last box of cucumbers in the bed of Meghan's truck and stepped back. When he turned around, he found her standing near the back door of the house, watching with a smile that sent warmth and longing racing through him. How he would love to set aside every tradition that had been ingrained in him from birth and all of the problems he had acquired since the Americans went into Afghanistan so that he could publicly show her affection. Yet his reservations, both cultural and personal, continued to hold him back. Perhaps after their date in the park he would find the courage to toss aside caution and hold her hand in public.

Memories rose of the day he had told her about the loss of his unborn child. The day he had been forced to admit his attraction to her. The touch of her fingers on his had been so gentle, so compassionate. And then when she allowed him to take hold of her hand...even now his heart raced just thinking about it.

Ryan slapped him on the back, intruding upon his reminiscence and bringing him back to the present. "Ready for your first date with my sister?"

"My first date ever," Basir corrected with a smile. "And yes, I am ready."

"Good. I need to go pick up Sara. See you at the park." Ryan headed for his car, giving his sister a wave.

Meghan joined Basir by the back of her truck and handed him a cooler. He set it beside the boxes of produce and closed the tailgate. As they climbed in the cab, he couldn't help an attack of nerves. Despite his assurance to Ryan only moments before, he wasn't sure he was ready for a date. In a short time, everyone at the park would know of his feelings for Meghan. If American towns were anything like Afghan villages, the rest of the population would know of his feelings in a day or two.

It felt as though he was publicly declaring his intentions to everyone but Meghan's father—the one man whose approval he needed if he ever wanted to marry her.

Meghan started the engine, but she turned to him before putting the truck in gear. "Everything OK?"

"Yes." Why couldn't he do a better job of hiding his thoughts?

"I don't believe you." She steered down the drive. "When are you going to realize you can tell me the truth and I won't ridicule you for it?"

"Forgive me." He wanted to beat himself for hurting her feelings. "Men in my country don't talk about our feelings."

She stopped at the end of the drive and turned toward him with compassion shining in her eyes. "Basir, I know. But you're in America now. You're on your way to becoming an American citizen. It's OK to talk about how you feel and to let others in. You don't have to keep everything hidden inside all the time."

He studied her while his head and his heart fought a familiar battle. Finally, he sighed and accepted the need to share his thoughts with her. "I am nervous about our date. I have never been on one before."

"I've been on several dates, but I'm nervous too." She smiled and gave his hand a quick squeeze. "It's perfectly normal, and I know we'll both have a great time."

"I am sure we will." Just knowing she wasn't as nonchalant as she seemed eased some of his worry about the evening.

They stopped at the town's grocery and parked by the back door. Basir helped one of the store's employees unload the produce while Meghan took care of the paperwork with the manager, and then they were on their way to the park. The parking lot was about half-full when they arrived, and Basir prayed he would have the courage to be the man Meghan wanted him to be. The man *he* wanted to be. The families scattered around the grass and playground sent longing through him. How he would love to bring his wife and children to the park for a picnic or just to relax on a nice afternoon. One day.

First, he had to survive a date with Meghan and hope it led to more dates in the coming weeks. He couldn't imagine sharing his life with anyone else, but he knew he had to follow the proper protocol for an American romance. That meant dates, meeting her family, and eventually asking her to marry him...or so he had been told by marines and healthcare workers.

Meghan pulled into an empty space beside her brother's car and shut off the engine. "It looks like Ryan and Sara have already picked out a spot for us. Let's grab the cooler and join them."

Basir scanned the area and spotted them sitting on a blanket beneath the shade of a large tree. Sara was digging in a cooler similar to the one Meghan had packed, and Ryan said something that made her laugh.

Basir dreamed of having such easy interaction with Meghan. The only reason their relationship was so much more reserved and awkward was because of him. If he would take a chance and attempt to be more outgoing with his feelings for her, maybe she would look at him the way Sara looked at Ryan.

Or maybe it would backfire horribly and ruin whatever relationship they had managed to build so far.

Sighing, he climbed out of the truck and retrieved the cooler from the back. One way or another, he needed to quit worrying about what could go wrong. Otherwise, he was liable to kill the relationship with his indecision and inaction.

God, give me strength and guidance.

Placing the situation in God's hands relieved a little of the pressure weighing him down, but not all of it. He still had to act—somehow. He just didn't know what to do yet.

~*~

"This is the perfect picnic spot," Meghan said as Basir set her cooler beside Sara's.

"You can thank Sara for it." Ryan shot an affectionate look toward his girlfriend. "She's the one who picked it out."

The blush in Sara's cheeks made Meghan wish Basir would look at her that way. How wonderful would it be to have him clearly announce his attraction to the world through a simple look or touch? But she had known going into the relationship that it wouldn't be like any she had ever experienced. Basir was a unique man with his own special set of obstacles to overcome. All she could do was encourage him and be patient as he navigated an unfamiliar world of romance.

Sara pulled a tray of sandwiches from her cooler. "I can't believe how long it's been since I went on a picnic."

"The closest thing to a picnic I've had recently is eating lunch in my booth at the farmer's market," Meghan said with a laugh. She followed Sara's lead and started unpacking the fresh veggies and brownies she'd brought.

The conversation over dinner remained light, focused mainly on the beautiful summer day and picnics of the past. Even Basir entered into the discussion with tales of picnics his family had gone on when he was a child. The innocuous story lightened Meghan's heart. It was the first thing she'd heard about his life in Afghanistan that didn't end with something devastating. Knowing he had happy memories to look back on warmed her.

After the meal, they packed the coolers, and the guys carried them back to the vehicles. Meghan braced her hands behind her and leaned back, looking up at the fading daylight filtering through the leaves.

"Basir's an unusual man, isn't he?" Sara's voice broke into her thoughts.

Meghan brought her gaze down and smiled. "Yes, he's different from anyone I've ever met."

"Is he always so...distant?"

"Not really. He's just shy and reserved, especially around women." She wasn't sure how much she should admit to Sara, but surely Ryan had told her at least that much.

"Doesn't that make it hard to have a relationship

with him?" Her face reddened. "I mean, Ryan's told me a little about the way things are in Afghanistan and that Basir's completely new to dating. He also warned me not to be surprised if Basir didn't talk to me or look at me at all. I didn't know if that same cultural stuff transferred over to his relationship with you or..."

The way she tried so hard to express her curiosity without being obviously nosy felt so familiar that Meghan had to laugh. How many times had she desperately wanted to give Basir the third degree just so she could understand *something* about him?

"Trust me, it can be awkward, but he's starting to relax around me." Meghan's gaze drifted to where the two men stood talking by the cars. "Honestly, there are times I wish he could be as relaxed with me as Ryan is with you."

Sara laughed, bringing Meghan's gaze back to her. "You should have seen your brother the first few times we talked. I was starting to think I terrified the poor man, but then he asked me out. Each time we talk or spend time together, he relaxes a little more. Now that he has a job, he's more relaxed than ever. Maybe it will work out the same way with Basir."

"It seems to be headed that way so far." Meghan's attention went back to the men, who were now approaching. Her brother, the confident marine who had never been shy in his life, had been that nervous about talking to Sara? It was hard to reconcile with what she remembered from before he deployed Afghanistan the first time, but she knew he had changed quite a bit since then. Apparently, whatever had caused him to need a safe place to readjust to civilian life had shaken his confidence more than she'd thought.

Ryan returned to his seat beside Sara, but Basir remained standing. Meghan looked up at him as he shifted his weight and briefly met her gaze.

"Would you like to take a walk with me?" he asked, his voice hesitant and heavily accented.

She smiled, hoping it would ease some of his nervousness. "I would love to."

As she shifted to stand, he held out a hand to her. Her breath caught in her throat, and she cast a quick glance at her brother. Ryan had a pleased expression on his face and nodded. Meghan took Basir's hand, and he helped her to her feet. Instead of letting go as she had expected, he kept hold of her hand as they headed for the paved walking trail around the perimeter of the park.

Meghan easily matched his leisurely pace and gave his hand a gentle squeeze. "This is nice."

"It is." He took a deep breath and slowly released it. "This is also scary. In Afghanistan, holding hands with a woman in public is grounds for punishment."

"Then it's a good thing we're not in Afghanistan." She smiled when he shot her a surprised look. "I'm proud of you for pushing past the fear and holding my hand anyway."

He flashed a brief smile and then faced the trail again. "Ryan has been encouraging me to act more like an American man. This is one small step in that direction, I hope."

"It is." She laid her head on his shoulder for just a second but straightened when she felt him tense. Even though he was doing better with public displays of affection, clearly he wasn't ready to move past hand holding.

They followed the path in companionable silence,

and Meghan breathed deeply, relaxing with each step. Spending time with a man who could appreciate quiet was a nice change from the dates Julia had arranged. Most of them seemed uncomfortable with any pause in the conversation.

"Meghan, I-I need to be honest with you." Basir's soft words sent a wave of nerves through her. Something about his tone threatened the peace of the afternoon.

"You know I appreciate honesty."

"I do, but..." He stopped them beside a huge oak, blocking them from Ryan and Sara's view. "I don't know if you will appreciate this."

"Regardless of what you have to say, I will appreciate the honesty of it, even if I don't like the words themselves." She prayed he wasn't going to dump her just when they were moving their relationship forward.

He nodded and then shocked her by grasping her other hand. No man so reserved around women would hold both her hands to dump her.

"You know there is no casual dating where I come from."

"Yes..."

"All marriages are arranged by the families. The bride and groom marry each other because their fathers tell them to, not because they met and fell in love."

"OK." Meghan's pulse raced faster than her mind. He wasn't going to propose to her on their first date, was he? She wasn't entirely sure she would insist on waiting to answer if he did.

"I want to get to know you better before marriage. I don't want to marry another woman without knowing her well and knowing she loves me."

"That's a good plan." Disappointment and relief warred within her. As much as she hadn't wanted him to propose so soon, part of her wanted that very thing. Then, what he said sank in. He wanted to get to know her before marriage? Maybe he planned to propose to her after all.

He looked across the park for a moment and then brought his gaze back to her. His eyes held more warmth than she had ever seen, and her heart took off on another gallop around her chest.

"I..." He drew in a breath and stepped closer to her, closer than he had ever been. "I know it is still early in our relationship, but I love you, Meghan."

Tears sprang to her eyes at the tenderness in his voice, and her heart overflowed. She desperately wanted to feel his arms around her, but she was afraid of upsetting him if she acted impulsively. "I love you, too, Basir. Would it be OK if I give you a hug?"

He smiled and nodded as he released her hands and spread his arms. She stepped into them, and he held her close. His warmth seeped into her as she slid her arms around his waist and leaned against him. The strength in his lean muscles made her feel safe and protected. The hesitant way he stroked a hand down her back made her feel cherished.

"You are a beautiful woman," he murmured in her ear. "Your beauty comes from within, shining out like a ray of sun on a stormy day."

She melted. Never would she have guessed that this man with a rough exterior and so many insecurities could be so poetic and romantic. She leaned back and looked him in the eye. "You have a beautiful soul. Despite all you have been through, you are one of the kindest, most caring men I have ever met."

His eyes misted, but he didn't say anything. Words were unnecessary. He hugged her tightly, conveying with his actions what spoken language could not express.

When he finally released her and stepped back, she keenly felt the loss of contact. The ache eased when he took her hand once more. They headed back to the blanket where Ryan and Sara still sat, but Meghan wished they were alone at the park. Now that she knew for sure how Basir felt, she wanted to bask in the warm glow of being loved by such a wonderful man. Never had she loved anyone as she loved Basir, and she had a feeling he had the same experience. Knowing he had been married once was a little intimidating, but from what he had said about his dead wife, she had no reason to worry she would fall short in any comparisons. All she had to worry about was how he would handle the stress of a romance and whether he would pull away from her again as he had done so many times before.

That worry could wait for another day, however. She planned to enjoy every minute of the new, outgoing Basir she could. Most likely he would become more reserved with her in a day or two, but at least now she could comfort herself with the knowledge that he loved her.

14

Each day, Basir's heart drew closer to Meghan. He knew that regardless of what he had said at the park, he would still want to marry her even if he took years to learn about her. He loved her.

Memories of the moment he confessed his love for her, the expression of pure joy that had come to her face, lightened his spirit and made him smile. Hearing she loved him as well had completed his love for her. All his concerns about things that mattered in Afghanistan but didn't matter in America faded away, leaving him able to accept that his honor wasn't ruined beyond repair. As Ryan and Meghan had both pointed out on numerous occasions, he was a good, honorable man in the eyes of Americans.

Now all he had to worry about was his lack of anything to offer Meghan other than himself. He had a feeling she wouldn't mind too much, but he didn't know if her parents would approve of him. Despite loving her, or maybe because he loved her, he wouldn't be able to marry her without her father's blessing. One of them without a family was enough. He wouldn't do anything to harm her relationship with her parents.

Soft humming reached his ears as he headed through the house toward the back door. Kadwaal stayed on his heels as he followed the sweet sound to Meghan's workshop. He peered into the room, and his heart thundered in his chest. She looked more beautiful than ever, preparing her workshop for a class she was conducting that afternoon. Her movements were so graceful as she separated an alpaca fleece into small piles at a long table she had set up in the middle of the room. Difficult though it was, Basir stepped away from the workshop doorway without letting her know he had ever been there and continued outside to check the alpacas' water supply.

Ever since the day she had voluntarily put on a long skirt just to make him more comfortable, he couldn't seem to stay away from her. That feeling had only grown stronger since their date in the park. Each moment he was near her brought a light to his soul he had been missing for years. Talking to her became easier as well. Ryan seemed pleased with his progress, but more importantly, Meghan's smile took on a new warmth whenever he conversed with her. When he held her hand or touched her cheek...Basir took a deep breath and prayed for God to give him the strength to keep his thoughts pure.

One day, hopefully soon, he wouldn't have to worry about it. But until they were married, if they did indeed marry, he intended to keep his thoughts and desires under tight control so as to refrain from disrespecting her in any way.

After he finished with the alpacas, he checked the garden. They would need to harvest again in the next day or two, but there were very few new invaders since the last time he weeded. He plucked a few tiny plants before they could take root and tossed them onto the path between rows. Kadwaal attacked them with gusto, and Basir chuckled.

"You will be a good hunter when you grow up.

Will you protect the house and barn from mice and rats?"

The kitten looked up at him and mewed, sounding as though he agreed with the assessment of his future abilities.

Basir leaned down and rubbed his head before scooping him up and cuddling him. "You are a smart one."

Kadwaal mewed again, and then settled down with a purr. The kitten had bonded tightly to Basir, but he didn't mind. Kadwaal made an excellent companion, and he got along well with the alpacas. He had grown like a weed since Basir first found him, easily regaining all of the weight he had been missing and developing a shiny, silky coat. Despite his shadow-like behavior, he had a sense of independence that found him regularly wandering off in search of adventure. He never strayed far from Basir, however, and always returned to him within a few minutes.

The crunch of tires on the driveway caught Basir's attention, and he looked up as an unfamiliar car approached the house. Two more turned into the drive, and he realized they must belong to Meghan's students. Still, to be sure she truly was safe, he headed for the house. By the time he stepped from the kitchen into the hallway with Kadwaal on his heels, Meghan was leading a pair of women, who appeared to be mother and daughter, into her workshop.

The doorbell rang, and Ryan came downstairs. He admitted three more women, ranging in age from mid-thirties to around sixty. As he guided them to the workshop, the doorbell rang once more.

"Can you get that, Basir?" Ryan asked. "It's probably one of Meghan's students."

When Basir opened the door, he found a pair of women who appeared to be in their late twenties or early thirties. They exchanged an uncertain glance, and then the one on the left spoke.

"Hi. We're here for the spinning class?"

"Come in." He stepped back and allowed them to enter. "The class is this way."

He led the two women down the hall and into Meghan's workshop. She looked up from the drop spindle she was fiddling with and smiled.

"Ah! The rest of my students! Have a seat here at the table, and we'll get started." She laid the spindle on the table and focused on Ryan and Basir. "Are you guys going to join the class?"

Basir glanced at Ryan, uncertain of how to answer. Did she want him there, or was she asking to be polite? Or maybe she asked simply as a way to prompt them to leave. Before he could decide which route would be best, the women in the room spoke up.

"Yes! You should stay."

"It would be so fun to have men in the class."

"The more the merrier, I always say."

The encouragement continued until Ryan blew out a breath. "All right! We'll stay. But I'll warn you. I already know how to use a drop spindle."

"If you get too bored, I can always turn you into an assistant." Meghan laughed. "Now, if you two will find places at the table, I'll get you some wool."

Basir took a seat at the end of the table and watched her gather the necessary supplies for two more students. He wasn't sure how to feel being in a class full of women, but at least he wasn't alone. Ryan was there to offer moral support and guidance if he needed it. Besides, he couldn't wait to see the woman he loved teaching others to do the craft she adored.

Once everyone had the necessary wool and equipment, Meghan stepped in front of the table. "In case you haven't already guessed, I'm Meghan Carpenter, owner of Carpenter Alpacas. Why don't you all introduce yourselves? We'll start with you."

The young woman at the end of the table gave the group a shy smile. "Hi. I'm Lila Porter."

The older woman with similar features sitting beside her spoke next. "I'm Lila's mother, Jane Porter."

Peggy Wallace came next, followed by Amanda Moore, Emily Kincaid, Heather Kline, and Kate Jackson. Ryan was next in line, and he leaned back in his chair as he spoke.

"I'm Meghan's brother, Ryan."

"My name is Basir." He tried not to notice the looks the women exchanged when he spoke, but it was impossible. Nearly every new person he had met in town had done the same thing the first time they heard his accent.

The kitten jumped on his lap and then onto the table and let out a loud meow. All the women laughed, and Basir smiled as he picked up his furry friend. "This is Kadwaal. He likes to be in the middle of everything."

He set the offended kitten on the floor and focused on Meghan as she started describing the process of preparing raw wool for spinning. The tools in front of him caught his attention and took him back to his childhood. Although his experience was with sheep wool, he had helped wash, pick, and card countless pounds of wool. The wool in front of him now had already been washed, according to Meghan, so he grabbed a glob of it and began to pick through it, loosening the fibers and removing any bits of debris that remained. He noticed Ryan doing the same thing as Meghan demonstrated the process for the others.

When Basir finished picking the wool, he grabbed one of the pin-filled paddles and carefully loaded some wool in an even layer. Then he picked up the matching carder and drew it across the wool-filled one, carding the wool so the fibers lined up with each other. As he worked, he caught Meghan watching him while she demonstrated the process he was already performing.

When he set aside the first carded bat of wool, she paused her lesson and turned toward him. "Has Ryan been teaching you how to do this in his spare time?"

"No, my mother taught me when I was a child." He didn't look at her as he added the next glob of wool to the carders. "My grandfather raised sheep, remember?"

"I do remember that. Do you know how to spin yarn too?"

"With a spinning wheel? No. With a drop spindle? Yes. That is how we spun all our yarn." He gave her a sheepish smile, uncomfortably aware that everyone was listening with rapt attention. "It has been a long time since I spun wool, so I may not be very good at it anymore."

"I'm sure you'll pick it up again in no time." Meghan's smile warmed him clear through, and then she returned her attention to her students.

Basir made quick work of carding the rest of his pile of wool. He wasn't surprised at how easily he fell into the rhythm of carding again. Kashmala had put him to work carding wool during the long winter so that she could focus on spinning yarn. He shoved aside the memory and focused on the task at hand. A quick glance to his right showed Ryan keeping pace with him. The women in the group weren't quite as fast, but it was clear none of them had experience working with wool.

By the time the female students had finished carding their small supply of wool, Basir and Ryan had moved on to spinning. Although rusty from years of not spinning, he soon picked up the skill again and created an even strand of yarn. Ryan started out spinning with the same ease as his sister, but he soon laid his spindle aside and went to help one of the women who was struggling. Meghan was working with the mother-daughter pair. Most of the others were doing all right, but the eldest woman in the group, Peggy, couldn't seem to get her yarn started.

After a moment of debate, Basir decided to use his newfound freedom from the old ways and stood. Meghan glanced at him as he stopped beside Peggy, and her smile gave him the courage he needed to speak.

"Would you like some help?"

"Oh, yes, please." She held up her spindle and a strip of carded wool. "I think this is on a mission to drive me batty."

"No, it just takes patience and practice." He demonstrated how to attach the wool to the starter string on the drop spindle. "Now you try it."

She did so with him guiding her through the process. When she finally managed to successfully spin her first few inches of yarn, she gave him a big smile. "You're an excellent teacher."

"Thank you." He returned to his seat and picked up his spinning where he had left off.

The repetitive motion soothed his nerves. Even

though he was more comfortable interacting with women, mostly thanks to Meghan's patient encouragement, he still couldn't relax as completely as Ryan. Perhaps one day, but helping Peggy with her spindle reminded him that he still had a long way to go.

~*~

Once the last student had paid for her purchase and left, Meghan breathed a sigh of relief. She loved teaching classes, but they always wore her out. The students inevitably asked dozens of questions about the yarn, the wool, the alpacas, and spinning in general as though they wanted to cram years of experience into just a few hours. At least this time, Ryan and Basir had been there to help with the spinning lesson and the brief tour of the farm. Having to answer every question herself was exhausting.

When she returned to her workshop, Basir was inside tidying up. Ryan had left for his job right after the tour. She watched Basir work for a moment, loving the way he seemed so at ease in her world. Most men had no clue what she did or how she did it, even after she explained it to them.

"Thank you," she said as she stepped further into the room. "I didn't expect you to help out today, but I'm glad you did."

He snapped the lid on a box of yarn. "You looked like you needed help, and I knew enough to be able to provide it."

She rested her hips against the edge of the table. "You know, Ryan was right when he said you're a good teacher. The way you helped Peggy was admirable."

He shrugged and joined her, leaning back against the table beside her. "You are an excellent teacher yourself."

"It wears me out, but I love it." She sighed and brushed her shoulder against his, pleased when he didn't move away. "I also love being able to include you in what I do around here. Not everyone gets it."

"I come from farmers and sheep farmers. What you do is so similar to the life I had before that it would be hard not to understand what you do." He slowly put his arm around her, almost as though he was afraid she would be upset. "But life here is not so hard. You do this because you want to, because you enjoy it, not because it is the only way to survive."

"True. If I failed at farming or my yarn business, I could always go get a job somewhere and still be able to support myself."

"But you would not be as happy as you are here."

"Also true." She leaned against him, and awareness raced through her as he held her closer. "What do you say to going out for dinner tonight? I really don't want to cook."

His sudden tension made her want to cry. She stepped out from under his arm and turned to face him.

"Basir, it's not a date or anything. Just two hungry people getting food."

"I know. I'm sorry." He combed his fingers through his thick hair. "Where do you want to go?"

"Anywhere with food I don't have to prepare." She laughed, hoping to lighten his mood.

He cracked a smile, but his tension remained. "Can we go somewhere other than the café downtown?"

"Sure. There's the pizza place at the edge of town, if that sounds good."

"Pizza is always good."

As they headed for her truck a little while later, she glanced at Basir, unable to contain her curiosity any longer. "Why don't you want to go to the café?"

"Ryan and I have gone there a few times. There is one woman who works there that is afraid of me. I don't want to deal with that tonight."

"Oh, I'm sure she's not afraid of you."

"She always hides in the kitchen while I am there."

"OK. Maybe she is scared of you." Meghan laid a hand on his shoulder. "I wouldn't worry about it too much if I were you. Small towns have their share of quirky people."

"I know, and I am not worried about it. I just feel uncomfortable when she hides."

"I don't blame you. So, let's go get some pizza and forget all our troubles."

Papa Marvin's Pizzeria was busier than Meghan had expected. She found an empty space in the crowded lot and prayed Basir would be able to enjoy his dinner. Memories of how nervous he always seemed in groups made her hesitate before climbing out of the truck.

"Since there are so many people here, would you rather order the pizza to go instead of eating here?"

"No." He looked toward the crowded restaurant and sighed. "This is a part of normal life. I want to be able to relax as much as you or Ryan in a situation like this, but I will never be able to do it if I avoid crowds."

"Good point." She reached over and gave his forearm a gentle squeeze, feeling the tension in his lean muscles. "I'll let you choose where we sit, and we'll leave any time you want to."

He turned toward her and placed his right hand over his heart in a gesture she hadn't seen in a while. "Thank you."

"You're welcome." She smiled and opened her door.

Basir met her at the front of the truck and walked beside her toward the restaurant's entrance. He made no move to reach for her hand or do anything else to show they were more than just friends. The lack of affection stung a little, but she comforted herself with a reminder that he was going to dinner with her in a crowded restaurant. With most people, it wouldn't be that big a deal, but Basir wasn't most people. Appearing with her in public without her brother or anyone else to act as a chaperone was huge.

Once they were seated at a small, out-of-the-way table that offered a clear view of the restaurant and had given their orders to the teenaged waitress, Basir leaned back in his chair and briefly met Meghan's gaze.

"It is hard to believe I am here with you."

"Why is that?"

"A few weeks ago, coming here even just as two hungry people getting food was too much for me to consider." He smiled and warmth filled his eyes. "Now I am here with the woman I love, in public, without a chaperone. Even though I still feel like someone is going to come and punish us, being here with you is very freeing."

"You've come a long way." She wanted to reach across the table and touch his hand or arm, but she had a feeling that would be too much for him. She settled for a smile and putting as much emotion into her eyes as she could. "I'm proud of you."

He shifted in his seat and looked away, leaving her uncertain. Had she said the wrong thing? Sent the wrong signal with her expression?

The waitress arrived before she had an answer. Basir didn't look at Meghan as he picked up a slice of the pepperoni pizza. She nibbled at a slice of her own as she waited for him to say something, but he seemed more interested in ignoring her existence than conversation. Finally, she couldn't take it anymore. She set her pizza on her plate and fought back tears.

"Basir, I'm sorry."

His gaze darted to her, and his eyebrows shot up. "Why? What did you do?"

"I don't know." She twisted the paper napkin in her lap and prayed for the strength and wisdom she needed. "I must have done something, though, because you're acting like I'm not even here. Whatever I did to make you mad, I'm sorry."

"I am not mad at you." He ducked his head and spoke so softly she barely heard him. "I am attracted to you."

More confusion piled on top of what already existed. "I know that. You told me a while ago. But what does that have to do with you suddenly not talking to me or looking anywhere near me?"

"Meghan..."

His struggle showed on his face, but she couldn't figure out what he was struggling with. Hadn't they already overcome everything that got in the way of their friendship?

He sighed and grabbed his glass of cola. After taking a long drink, he finally looked at her. The heat smoldering in his eyes surprised her and sent tingles chasing along her spine.

"The way you looked at me when you told me you are proud of me..." He blew out a breath and looked away again. "You are a beautiful woman, and I love you. But we are not married. We are not even engaged. I must remember that, no matter how difficult it may be at times."

Her heart skipped a beat as his mention of marriage, but she couldn't focus on that. "So, I made you uncomfortable?"

"Yes, but it was not exactly bad." His cheeks turned a ruddy color, leaving her to wonder just what had gone through his mind.

Since he had specifically mentioned needing to remember they weren't married, perhaps it was better if she didn't know.

As she searched for a way to change the topic to something light, Julia stopped by their table.

"Meghan, Basir, it's good to see you!" Her smile grew wider as she turned to Meghan. "Enjoying a cozy dinner, I see."

Basir looked as if he wanted to sink beneath the table, but Meghan wouldn't give Julia the satisfaction of such a reaction. She laughed lightly and shook her head. "I think you need to look around. This place is hardly cozy."

"The place may be crowded, but I notice your brother isn't with you." Julia sent a pointed look at the two plates on the table.

"He's at work." Meghan could feel the discomfort rolling off Basir in waves and decided to take pity on him. "So, are you here with your husband?"

"Yes. Henry is waiting for our order." Julia patted Meghan's shoulder. "But I saw you and just had to come say hi."

"Well, it was good to see you."

Julia didn't take the hint. "Oh! You had a spinning class today, didn't you? How did that go?"

"We had a lot of fun. Ryan and Basir joined in and helped out. They both did a great job when several of my students had trouble at the same time."

"Really? I knew you taught your brother to use a drop spindle, but I hadn't realized you taught Basir as well."

"I didn't. His mom did when he was a kid."

"How fascinating." Julia turned to Basir, who had managed to regain his usual impassive expression. "You must have the most interesting tales to tell, being from Afghanistan and all."

Basir shrugged and didn't look at her. "My only tales are just life where I come from."

"True, but I'm sure life over there is quite different from life here."

"It is." He fell silent, but the look he sent Meghan left no doubt in her mind that he was ready for the conversation to end.

Before she could find a graceful way to tell Julia to go elsewhere, her husband called to her from near the entrance. She waved a hand in his direction. Then she focused on Meghan and sighed.

"That's my cue to leave. You two enjoy the rest of your dinner. I'll see you around!"

As soon as she walked away, Basir released a breath. Meghan studied him, wondering what had made him so uncomfortable. Tired of wondering all the time and receiving very few explanations, she decided to take a risk.

"Can I ask you something?"

"Of course." His gaze grew intense, and she felt as though she was the only person in the room with him.

Warmth filled her heart. "I could tell you were really uncomfortable with Julia stopping to talk. What caused that? I mean, is it just that whole men not talking to women thing, or the fact that she found the two of us in public alone, or...?"

"It is a little of both. There are many things I am still trying to adjust to, and tonight has brought several of them in front of me." He picked up his glass, but he didn't drink from it. Instead, he appeared to study the contents as he spoke quietly. "Now that someone close to you has seen us together in public without a chaperone, there is no chance of keeping our relationship a secret."

"Is that so bad?" She tried not to let his words hurt her feelings, but it was a difficult task.

"No. Not at all." He returned his glass to the table and met her gaze. "It's just that I have not talked to your father yet. I don't know if he will approve of me, and I can't help thinking he will be angry that I developed a relationship with you before talking to him."

Her heart broke for him. How difficult must life be to live under the constant worry of doing the wrong thing and offending someone? "Basir, you have nothing to worry about. My dad is a nice guy, like Ryan. And Ryan knows you better than anyone. He'll tell our dad that you're a good man."

"But it still feels like I am sneaking around with you since I haven't spoken with him yet."

"I'm sure it does simply because of the way you were raised, but you're not sneaking around. This is the normal, American way of romance. Two people meet, get to know each other, and fall in love. Then, they meet each other's families. There's no permission needed."

"I know that in my head, but in my heart..." He sighed and shook his head. "It is hard."

"I know." She wished she could make the transition to American life easier for him, but it was something he would have to work through on his own. "Instead of worrying about all of that right now, why don't we finish our pizza and get out of here? I'm sure you'll find it easier to relax back at the farm."

He nodded, and they continued their dinner in silence. This time, Meghan didn't try to encourage him to talk. His silence had nothing to do with her. Rather, it was the same silence she had witnessed many times as her brother worked through things in his own mind. She had a feeling that silence was something she would have to get used to. With everything in Basir's past, it could easily take a lifetime or more to work through it all.

15

The echo of children's laughter filled the church hall, and Basir watched as a group of kids around eight or ten years old played in one corner of the room. He wished he still had their innocence, but he had lost it long ago due to circumstances beyond his control. All he could do now was move forward and pray God would give him the strength to face whatever obstacles lay ahead.

Meghan joined him and handed him a foam cup filled with coffee. "You look like you're thinking some deep thoughts."

He shrugged and took a sip of the bitter brew. "I was just thinking how nice it must be to grow up somewhere like the United States."

"As someone who grew up here, I think I can safely say it's a pretty good place to be a kid."

Ryan approached with another church member at his side. "Hey, I have great news. Ken, here, has a two-bedroom apartment for rent at a very reasonable price."

Basir hoped Ryan meant the second bedroom for him. No way could he continue to live on Meghan's farm once Ryan moved out. Not only would it be inappropriate, he feared the temptation would be too great without someone else living in the house to act as a buffer.

"Are you going to take it?" Meghan asked.

"I'm thinking about it." Ryan glanced at Ken. "This is Basir Hamidi, the roommate I told you about."

"It's good to meet you, Basir," Ken said with a friendly smile. "Ryan tells me you two met during one of his deployments in Afghanistan."

"Yes, I was an interpreter for the marines." Sharing that bit of information with strangers grew easier all the time. "Ryan and I worked together often on his last four deployments."

"Well, I appreciate the service you did." Ken exchanged a look with Ryan, and then focused on Basir once more. "Like I already told Ryan, I'm going to give you guys a military discount. Instead of requiring first and last month's rent like I usually do for new tenants, I'm only asking for your first month's rent."

That explained how Ryan was able to afford an apartment so soon after starting his job. Basir placed his right hand over his heart and smiled. "Thank you."

"It's not much, but it's the least I can do to thank you for the sacrifices you made."

"Ken says we can look at the apartment this afternoon if we want," Ryan said, his excitement over the idea evident in his eyes. "What do you say?"

"If you want to look at it this afternoon, I will go with you."

"Cool."

Ryan and Ken wandered off, talking about when to see the apartment. Basir glanced at Meghan and found her looking sad.

"What's wrong?" Maybe he shouldn't have agreed to go with her brother that afternoon, but he couldn't figure out how that would upset her.

"Oh, nothing." She forced a smile that didn't reach her eyes.

"You are a terrible liar, Meghan." He faced her fully and looked her in the eye long enough to make himself uncomfortable. "Why do you look sad when your brother is so excited?"

"I'm happy for him and everything. I mean, I know he's been wanting to get out on his own again for a while, but..." She sighed and shook her head. "I've gotten used to you guys sharing my house. It's going to be lonely with just me out there."

"You will still see us." He wanted to give her a hug, to reassure her he would always be there for her, but he couldn't do it. Not in such a public place. He settled for touching her arm and smiling. "I still work for you, remember? Even though I will live somewhere else, I will be on your farm every day to care for the alpacas and to help with anything else."

The light that came to her eyes warmed his heart. "I hadn't thought about that. Maybe I won't be so lonely after all. I'll still miss you guys, though."

He debated making an offer. Ryan likely wouldn't mind, but would it be appropriate? Thinking back over what the marines had said and Ryan's own actions, he could only assume it would be. "If you get too lonely, maybe you could come visit us."

"That could work. We'll have plenty of time to figure it out, I'm sure." She released a breath and tilted her head at an inquisitive angle. "By the way, do you know how to drive? I mean, since you're going to be living in town, you'll need a way to get out to the farm. I don't mind driving you, and I'm sure Ryan won't either, but it would be easier if you could drive yourself."

Some of his good mood evaporated under the harsh glare of reality. "I can't drive."

"Well, I'm sure you could learn."

He shook his head and focused on the far wall as he struggled to remember that the challenges he faced didn't lessen his worth as a man. "No, the doctors said I can't drive. I don't know if that will ever change, but for now..."

"I'm sorry, Basir." Meghan laid her hand on his arm. "I didn't think."

"There is no way you could have known." He met her gaze, and the sympathy he found there threatened to do him in. "I am luckier than many with traumatic brain injuries, but it still interferes with life sometimes."

She reached out and gave his hand a squeeze that set his heart racing. A quick glance around showed no one giving them disapproving looks. No one appeared to notice at all. Maybe holding her hand in public wouldn't be so bad.

The congregants moved toward the exit, indicating it was almost time for the worship service. Basir took a chance and kept hold of Meghan's hand as they followed along. She smiled warmly and walked a little closer to him, making it clear she approved of the move. He caught Ryan watching from across the room, but he had no need to worry. His friend grinned and nodded then went on his way.

As they headed down the hallway, Meghan leaned close and whispered, "You're getting brave."

He chuckled and grasped her fingers a little more firmly. "I can't live in fear forever. And as you and Ryan like to remind me, we are in America where the rules are different."

"I'm glad you're finally taking advantage of them. I could get used to this."

Basir didn't respond, but one thought bounced around his mind.

He could get used to it too.

~*~

Meghan joined Basir and her brother at the front of the car. Ryan didn't seem to notice his friend's apprehension, yet she couldn't ignore it. The café was busier than usual with the after-church crowd, but she knew that wasn't Basir's real issue. Was the woman who feared him working today, or would he get a break from the discomfort of having her hide from him?

Taking Basir's hand, Meghan spoke softly. "It'll be OK."

"I know." He sighed and shook his head. "It is her problem, not mine."

"If it helps, you can sit with your back to the kitchen."

Basir nodded, but Ryan interrupted before he could speak. "Hey, Sara!"

Meghan looked down the street and spotted the brown-haired woman approaching with a smile. "You invited your girlfriend?"

"Sure." Ryan glanced at her. "Why not?"

"No reason." She refused to admit how interesting she found it that Sara was joining them for lunch and presumably to look at the apartment afterwards. To Meghan, it sounded as if the relationship was much more serious than Ryan had let on. But since he wanted to pretend it was no big deal, she would let him. She knew that method worked to keep Basir more comfortable, so maybe it worked for her brother too.

Ken arrived and the group entered the café. A young woman wearing an apron paused as she carried a tray past.

"Welcome! There's an empty table over there." She nodded toward the middle of the right wall. "If you'll go have a seat, I'll be right with you to take your order."

She continued on her way, and the group walked toward the vacant table. As Ryan pulled out a chair for Sara, Meghan heard a quiet sigh beside her. She glanced at Basir and found him gazing toward the back. A quick glance in that direction showed an older woman disappearing through the swinging door to the kitchen. A second later, the door reopened a crack and she peered out, looking directly at Basir before ducking out of sight again.

No wonder he didn't like going to the café. She wouldn't either with someone acting like that.

Meghan took his hand and gave it a gentle squeeze. "Ignore her."

He nodded and then pulled out the chair across the table from Sara. Meghan sat down, and he took the seat beside her. Ryan settled next to Sara, and Ken took a chair at the end, facing both couples. They passed around the laminated menus from the holder on the table and studied them while they waited for the waitress to arrive.

Ken's gaze kept drifting toward the back of the restaurant, and finally he said, "What on earth is she doing?"

Ryan looked up from his menu. "What is who doing?"

"Sandra keeps peeping out of the kitchen like she's expecting an invasion." Ken shook his head. "I know she's been a little strange since her son's friend got killed in Afghanistan, but this is weird even for her."

A sharp intake of breath sent Meghan's attention to Basir. He glanced over his shoulder, an understanding expression on his face. Then he faced Ken and spoke quietly. "I think she is afraid of me. She does this every time I come here."

"Hmm." Ken studied him then looked toward the kitchen once more. "I think it's time she meets you. I'll be right back."

As soon as he left the table, Basir focused on Ryan. "Is this a good idea?"

"Yes. You don't want her to remain scared of you for no reason. Now, if you want to give her a reason to be scared, that's different."

Meghan rolled her eyes. "You're a dork, Ryan."

"You're just now figuring that out?"

"Nope. I've known it for years. You just need to be reminded every now and then so you don't forget."

Sara laughed and shook her head. "You guys are hilarious."

Ryan put his arm around her and leaned close. "I'm glad you can appreciate it."

Ken returned with the woman from the kitchen. She looked ready to jump out of her skin, but he pulled her closer to the table.

"Sandra Baker, this is Basir Hamidi, Ryan Carpenter, Ryan's sister, Meghan, and Sara Gotheridge. Sandra is my cousin's ex-wife," Ken said. "Ryan and Basir are hopefully going to be renting from me."

"Hello," Sandra said, her wide eyes on Basir.

"It is good to meet you." He glanced at Meghan as if seeking reassurance, and then he spoke to Sandra again. "I am very sorry to hear about your son's friend. I know what it is like to have someone close to you killed by the Taliban."

"Tha-thank you." Something in her eyes changed, and some of the fear rolling off her faded. She took a deep breath and pulled a pad from the pocket of her apron. "Have you guys ordered?"

"Not yet," Ken said as he returned to his seat.

After taking their orders, she returned to the kitchen. Ken smiled at Basir. "I'll probably be answering a ton of questions the next time I talk to her, but she should stop hiding from you now."

"Thank you." Basir placed his hand over his heart. "I don't like for people to fear me."

"I wouldn't either."

The conversation moved on, and Meghan reached for Basir's hand under the table. He grasped her fingers and met her gaze with a faint smile. Her heart skipped a beat, and she said a quick prayer of thanks. Not only for Sandra no longer hiding from him, but also for his newfound ability to show small bits of affection in front of other people. He had grown so much in the time she had known him, and he had taught her so much about what a relationship could be.

Now she had to hope that the connection they had worked so hard to build would survive after he moved off the farm.

16

Basir set a box on the living room floor by the end of the couch and straightened with a sigh. His back ached from the exertion of moving boxes and furniture, but it felt good. For the first time in years, he had a safe home to call his own. During a lengthy conversation after seeing the two-bedroom apartment above one of the stores downtown, Ryan had assured him the apartment would belong to both of them for however long they wanted to live there. Even though Basir couldn't completely pay his way, he was able to contribute enough thanks to his job on Meghan's farm to feel like he was finally supporting himself again.

The sense of being a self-sufficient man once more lifted a weight from his shoulders and allowed him to have hope for the future.

Meghan entered the apartment with a box in her arms, and Basir quickly relieved her of the burden.

"Thanks." She smiled and wiped a loose strand of hair from her eyes. "Ryan's bringing up the last box."

"OK."

He hadn't been sure about allowing her to help with moving, but she had insisted and Ryan backed her up. Maybe one of these days having women do heavy work like farming and moving furniture would seem normal, but for now, Basir still wished he could keep Meghan from having to do anything other than care for her home and make her yarn. Even though he couldn't make life that simple for her, he planned to do as much as he could around the farm to ease her workload. Doing so much work also gave him a convenient excuse to spend large amounts of time near her. Not seeing her from morning until night was the only drawback to moving into town, but he couldn't have continued living in her house. Not without a chaperone.

Not yet.

He pushed aside thoughts of the future and carried the box to his bedroom. After setting it on the floor, he looked around the room he could truly call his. A twin bed stood against the wall to the right of the door. Across from the door, a scarred wooden dresser topped with a mirror sat against the wall. A closet occupied the opposite wall, and the fourth held a window overlooking the street below. In the corner by the window, a plain wooden armchair with dark blue cushions sat waiting for him to practice reading or relax with his kitten in his lap. Many Americans would likely consider the room sparse, but he liked the simplicity of little furniture or decoration. It felt like home.

Leaving his room, he looked down the short hall ahead of him. Ryan's room stood at the end. A closet opened off the side left, and the bathroom stood on the right. When Basir turned left, he was back in the large living room where Ryan now stood with Meghan between the coffee table and the entertainment center. Another turn to the left would take him into the small kitchen dominated by a plain wooden table and four chairs, while going straight would send him to the front door. The apartment wasn't huge, but it was big enough for two men to share comfortably.

"It's all in," Ryan said. "All that's left is going back to Meghan's and picking up Kadwaal."

"I can do that if you want," Meghan said, shifting her gaze to Basir. "You're welcome to come with me. Kadwaal might appreciate it, since you're his human."

Basir's heart melted at the sound of the kitten's Pashto name rolling off her tongue. Her pronunciation had improved immensely in the last few weeks, and she almost had the accent down. A discreet cough from Ryan brought him out of his musing, and for once he made a quick decision rather than thinking too hard about what would be proper. "I will go with you."

"Great!" A smile lit up Meghan's face, and Basir knew he had made the right choice.

"I'll go pick up a pizza for our dinner and meet you guys back here," Ryan said, heading for the door.

Basir was the last one out, so he locked the door before following Meghan downstairs. Her truck sat at the curb, right behind her brother's car. He climbed into the passenger seat as she settled behind the wheel. Once they were on the road, he spoke.

"Thank you for helping us move into our apartment."

"I was glad to do it. You guys have helped me so much since moving in, the least I could do is offer my truck and my hands to help you move out."

He looked out the windshield as he considered the wistful note in her voice. It echoed the feeling in his heart. "I am going to miss sharing a house with you."

"I'm going to miss you too." She held out her hand, and he grasped it. "It's been a while since I lived alone. I'm going to have to adjust to not having other people around all the time."

He rubbed his thumb across her knuckles,

enjoying the little shiver he felt run through her. "I will be on your farm every day to care for the alpacas and do whatever you need me to do."

"I know, but it's not the same." She sighed as she braked for a stop sign, and then she glanced at him. "I don't want you to feel guilty for moving or like you're abandoning me or anything like that. Even though I'm going to miss having housemates, I'm really happy for you guys. I can tell you're both happier with a space of your own. We'll all adjust to living in separate places, and it will make those times we are together that much sweeter."

Her smile was sweet enough to muddle his thinking. Unable to resist, he lifted her hand and kissed the back. Her surprised gasp and the blush that stole across her cheeks let him know taking the risk had been worth it.

His courage bolstered by her reaction, he said, "We should go out sometime."

"Are you asking me on a date?" She glanced at him with wide eyes and then focused on the road once more.

"Yes." He couldn't deny it when the truth was so obvious, and he had a feeling she didn't mind his newfound boldness. In fact, she seemed to enjoy it. "So, would you like to go out with me?"

"I would love to." The gentle pressure of her fingers against his sent his pulse racing.

"How does next weekend sound? Maybe Saturday?"

"It will have to be later in the afternoon or the evening. Next Saturday is my farmer's market day." She pulled her hand from his to navigate a turn. "What are we going to do?"

"What do you want to do?"

"If the weather cooperates, we could have a picnic dinner at the park." She sent a shy smile his way. "I really enjoyed our last date there."

"So did I." He could still barely believe he had admitted his love for her. Even more stunning was that she had accepted it and confessed her love for him as well.

He wasn't sure how much longer he could refrain from having a serious discussion with her about marriage. He had dropped a few hints already, but she hadn't said anything other than to agree getting to know the person before you married was important. Maybe another walk through the park would be the perfect time to bring up the subject of marriage again.

A little voice in the back of his mind insisted he was going about it the wrong way—that he should be talking to her father before anyone else. But he was in America now, and it was past time he started doing things the American way rather than the Afghan way.

~*~

Meghan paused in winding her latest batch of yarn and looked out the window. The gorgeous summer day begged to be enjoyed, but she had to finish winding the yarn into skeins so she could sell it at the farmer's market the next day. If Basir was there, she might be tempted to abandon her yarn and go outside anyway, but he and Ryan both had appointments at the VA clinic that morning. They would be over sometime after lunch to help pick the produce for the farmer's market. She planned to finish with the yarn before then so she could be outside enjoying their company.

As she went back to work, her thoughts drifted over the last week of living on her own. She had adjusted to the absence of her housemates faster than she'd expected. Part of it had to do with Ryan dropping Basir off before breakfast every morning. While he cared for the alpacas, she cooked. Then he came in, and they shared the meal while discussing the rest of the day's work. Ryan had stopped by for lunch or dinner a few times, but he was busy with his job and Sara. That meant most of the time Meghan and Basir were on their own until she took him home in the evening.

The time they spent together had brought them closer, and Meghan could see Basir's confidence grow every day. He still hadn't done anything more affectionate than hold her hand, except for the day she'd helped him move and he kissed her hand. That moment was burned into her memory, and she couldn't wait for their second date. Maybe he would finally kiss her, but even if he didn't, she was thrilled to be going out on their first official date without a chaperone.

Looking back over their relationship so far, she was amazed at how far they had come since Ryan first brought Basir into her life. The shy, timid man who wouldn't look at her and barely spoke to her had been replaced by a confident man who held her hand and talked to her with ease. She had changed as well. Since meeting Basir, she had learned to be calmer, quieter inside. Her patience had been tested and strengthened, and even her clothing had changed. In her attempt to make Basir more comfortable around her, she had discovered a style that made her more comfortable as well. Gone were the shorts and tank tops that had once been staples in her summer wardrobe. She had replaced them with long skirts, jeans, and T-shirts, a change that when combined with Basir's appreciative looks made her feel more feminine and cherished than ever.

She finished with the yarn and packed it into a box. With it still too early for lunch, she headed out to the garden to face the never-ending task of weeding. No matter how many weeds she pulled, new ones always popped up to take their place.

As she worked her way down the first row, she heard a car on the drive. Ryan and Basir must have decided to join her for lunch. She kept working, certain they would come find her soon enough. When she heard two sets of footsteps rounding the house, she straightened and turned toward them.

"Hey, you guys are—" Her heart thundered in her chest at the sight of two strangers in green-and-khaki uniforms. "Not who I expected. Can I help you?"

"I hope so." The older of the two men removed his hat as he stopped at the edge of the garden. "Are you Meghan Carpenter?"

"Yes..." A sense of dread settled in the pit of her stomach. Even though Ryan was no longer serving and was safe, she had spent so long fearing a visit like this. Two uniformed men arriving to tell her something terrible had happened to her brother. Never mind that the rational part of her knew they would have gone to her parents' house, not hers. The fear had still lingered, and these two visitors brought it back full force.

"I'm Colonel Jamar Spencer. Your brother, Ryan, served under me."

"It's good to meet you." Meghan left the garden

and joined him, hoping he would soon get to the point of his visit. Otherwise, she was liable to burst into tears or scream.

"I heard Ryan is living here now. Is he home?"

"He did live here, but he moved into town last weekend. He has an apartment above the hardware store." She wrapped her arms around her middle as her heart sent up a continuous stream of prayer. "Is everything OK?"

"Oh, yes. Everything is fine." Spencer gave her a reassuring smile. "I didn't mean to make you worry. In fact, I'm not even here to see your brother. I'm looking for his friend Basir Hamidi. Rumor has it he's staying here too."

"He was, but he moved into Ryan's apartment."

"I see." Spencer motioned his companion over. "This is Lance Corporal Adams. Would you mind giving him your brother's new address?"

She recited the address and watched the young man no older than twenty-one write it down in a small notebook. Why was the colonel looking for Basir? Had something fallen through with his green card? Were they deporting him? Did they want him to go back to being an interpreter?

The thought of him going back to Afghanistan for any reason terrified her. She had a feeling he wouldn't make it out alive again.

"Thank you, Miss Carpenter," Spencer said, replacing his hat on his head. "We'll be on our way."

She watched the two men leave as suddenly as they had appeared. A moment later, she heard their car go back up the drive. Unfortunately, her fear didn't follow them. It remained strong in her heart as she prayed harder than ever for Basir's safety.

~*~

Lunch held little appeal after Colonel Spencer's visit, but Meghan forced herself to eat anyway. Regardless of why the colonel was looking for Basir, she had a farm to run and a farmer's market to prepare for. Both tasks took a tremendous amount of energy, and she needed to keep her body well-fueled if she wanted to complete them successfully. Since her livelihood depended on her success, she made a sandwich and sat down at the table with it and a glass of ice water.

She finished the last bite and carried her dishes to the sink. Before she could wash them, she heard the front door. Relief flooded her. Everything had to be fine if her brother and Basir had arrived right on time. Stepping into the hall, she spotted only her brother.

"Where's Basir?" she asked with a sinking feeling.

"He packed a bag and went with Colonel Spencer." Ryan grinned, making her want to strangle him for his nonchalance. "By the way, both the colonel and Lance Corporal Adams said you're cute."

"Great. It's nice to know I can still impress marines just by being alive." She rolled her eyes despite her worry. How many times had the men her brother served with hit on her or made some comment about her looks?

He laughed, appearing completely unconcerned that the Marine Corps had just hauled away his best friend. "I think Adams wishes he could have hung around a little longer just so he could get to know you."

"Too bad for him I'm already taken." She drew in

a deep breath, hoping to calm her nerves. "Do you know where they took Basir?"

"Nope. But I'm sure they'll bring him back soon enough." Ryan walked past her toward the kitchen. "So, what are we doing first? Picking produce or working on the weeding Colonel Spencer mentioned you doing?"

Meghan sighed and followed him. Clearly her brother wasn't going to discuss the situation with Basir any further. "Let's finish the weeding. It's still a little early to work on the produce."

As they worked their way through the garden, Meghan wanted to cry. She felt the loss of Basir so deeply, and the lack of information on where he had gone and for how long scared her. Ryan's calm demeanor gave her a glimmer of hope that nothing bad would happen to the man she loved, but she needed to know what was going on in order to fully trust he would be safe. Then there was the fact that she had no idea when he would return. Would he miss her while he was gone? Would he still want her when he returned?

Why hadn't he called to let her know what was going on?

Her heart ached with the realization he hadn't called. Wasn't that what a man did when he loved a woman? Called to let her know he was going away for a few days or longer? With his rural upbringing in rather primitive conditions, she couldn't discount the possibility that calling her hadn't even occurred to him. But surely he would have had the presence of mind to give Ryan a message for her—unless he didn't love her as much as he claimed.

"Father God," she whispered, thankful her brother

was working a few rows away and couldn't hear her. "Help me to trust Basir's love. Help me to trust that You will keep him safe and bring him back in one piece. And, Lord, please help me to stay calm and be patient while I wait for his return. I know worrying won't help, but it's hard not to worry when the man I love is picked up by the marines and taken to an unspecified location for an indeterminate length of time. I know You are with him and me both, but I have a feeling it's going to be a long wait for him to get back. Please help me survive the wait with a minimal amount of freaking out."

She blinked away tears as she reached for another weed. Even knowing God was looking out for Basir and would give her comfort, she couldn't shake the fear that something bad would happen. How would she survive the heartache of losing the man she wanted to spend her life with?

Her vision blurred once more at the thought of never seeing Basir again, and she sighed. Yes, it would be a very long wait indeed.

17

Saturday morning lasted an eternity as Meghan faked smiles and engaged in cheerful small talk when all she wanted to do was cry. All around her, the farmer's market bustled. Yet she was alone, wondering if she would ever hear from Basir again.

She had tried several times the previous evening to get more information out of her brother, but Ryan wouldn't tell her anything. Finally, he had threatened to leave her to finish picking produce on her own if she didn't stop asking him things he couldn't answer. She acquiesced, but she couldn't shake a new question. Why couldn't her brother answer her seemingly simple questions about where Basir had gone and for how long? Was it because he didn't know, or had Colonel Spencer sworn him to secrecy?

The uncertainty had plagued her all night, and now she had to pretend that everything was fine so she had a chance of selling everything she had brought with her.

She added a few more cucumbers to the display and smiled at the passing people. Someone approached the booth as she straightened the tomatoes, and she prepared to convince the latest customer to buy some produce. Turning toward the newcomer, her stock greeting died in her throat.

"Sara, hi! I didn't expect to see you today." Meghan's face heated. "I mean, Ryan's at work, so..."

Sara laughed and stepped closer. "I understand. I'm actually here to buy a few things. Ryan's coming over for dinner tonight, and I know he would enjoy eating from your garden."

"My brother got spoiled living with me," Meghan said with a smile. "I've been sending fresh veggies home with Basir most days since they moved out."

Sara picked up a pair of cucumbers. "Where is Basir? I'm surprised he's not here helping you."

"He had to go out of town." Meghan adjusted some of the herbs and tried not to think about how far out of town he might have gone.

"Oh? Is he going to be gone long?"

"I'm not sure. According to Ryan, he'll be back soon enough." Meghan sighed and met Sara's curious gaze. "I didn't have a chance to talk to Basir before he left."

"Weird. I would have thought he would call you."

"Basir rarely does what I would expect from an American man." And she loved him for all his quirks and strange behavior. Even so, she couldn't help wishing that for once he would have done the American thing and either called her while he packed or once he arrived wherever Colonel Spencer took him.

"He certainly is unique." Sara's laugh faded as she studied Meghan. "Wait a minute. I thought Ryan said something about you and Basir going out tonight."

"We were supposed to, but then he had to leave." Meghan shook her head and commanded herself not to cry. "I guess we'll just have to postpone our date until he gets back."

"After you waited so long for him to finally ask you out?" Sara set down the produce she had collected and reached for Meghan's hands. "I can't imagine how hard that must be. Why don't you come to my house for dinner?"

Meghan's heart lifted a little at this show of caring from her brother's girlfriend, yet she couldn't help feeling guilty at the invitation. "I don't want to ruin your date."

"You won't. It's not really a date, anyway." Sara grinned and gave her hands a gentle squeeze. "Mainly, Ryan didn't want to have to cook tonight, and I never object to the opportunity to spend time with him."

"Well, I guess I could join you." She hoped her brother wouldn't mind her being a third wheel, but it was Sara's house.

"Great!" Sara released her hands and looked over the produce once more. "Now, I just need a few more things. We're having lasagna and salad."

Meghan helped her find what she needed, and then bagged it up. When Sara tried to pay, Meghan refused to take the money. "It's on me. Consider it a thank you for keeping me from having a lonely Saturday night."

"Well, if you're sure..."

"I am." Meghan leaned closer and lowered her voice. "Between you and me, sales are slow today. I'm likely to end up hauling a lot of this home, so whatever goes with you is that much less I have to pack up at the end of the day."

Sara laughed and nodded. "All right, then."

After providing her address, Sara wandered off. Meghan went back to trying to entice people to buy her products. Some weeks she sold out quickly, but days like this one left her glad her yarn business was a large part of her income. By the end of the market, she still had more than she liked to carry home. As she packed, she loaded a couple of plastic bags with produce to take with her to Sara's. Ryan could take one home, and Sara could have the other. Even after separating those vegetables out, she still had two and a half boxes to figure out something to do with. She might give them to friends at church or make casseroles or other items that could be frozen. If enough of it was in good shape on Monday, she could drop it off at the food pantry.

By the time she unloaded her truck at home and stored everything, she barely had time to change into a long summer dress. Then she was back in her truck and heading for Sara's small house a few blocks from downtown. Ryan's car sat in the drive behind an older compact car, so Meghan parked at the curb. She grabbed the two bags of produce and climbed out. As she walked up the path lined with cheerful flowers, the front door opened, and Ryan stepped out.

"Hey, sis. Come on in."

"Thanks." She paused before stepping through the doorway and looked at him. "I hope you don't mind me being here. Sara insisted I wouldn't be in the way, but—"

"She's right. I should have thought of it myself." He slung an arm around her shoulders and guided her inside. The warm scents of tomato sauce and baked cheese surrounded them. "I know you're worried about Basir and upset that your date with him has to be postponed. Leaving you on your own tonight would be wrong."

"I don't know about that, but I am glad to have company."

Ryan gave her a hug, and then stepped away to close the door. When he turned around, he gestured toward the bags in her hands. "Sara didn't say anything about you contributing to dinner."

"I'm not. It wasn't a good day at the farmer's market, and I have to do something with the leftovers." Meghan handed him the bags. "There's one for you and one for Sara."

"Thanks."

She followed him through a tidy living room with a tan couch, a metal-and-glass coffee table, and an upholstered chair in the back corner with packed bookshelves on either side. They stepped into a nice-sized kitchen with pale sage walls and white cabinets and countertops. Off to one side stood a white-and-light wood table and matching chairs. A window above the sink showed a backyard blooming with flowers.

Sara turned from the white gas stove and smiled. "Hi, Meghan! I'm just about to cut the lasagna."

"It smells delicious."

Ryan joined his girlfriend and held up the bags. "She brought us some produce."

"You didn't have to do that!" Sara smiled as she peeked into the bags and then set them on the counter. "But I do appreciate it. Thank you."

"You're welcome." Meghan didn't bother explaining the poor sales again. Ryan could tell her if he wanted.

"Ryan, could you get the salad out of the fridge?" Sara said as she turned back to her work.

"Sure thing." He moved to the appliance in the corner, completely at ease in Sara's kitchen.

A pang hit as Meghan watched her brother and his girlfriend move around the kitchen, setting the table and finishing last-minute details on the meal. It reminded her so much of the last week with Basir in her own kitchen. He had been growing progressively more comfortable in the domestic setting, helping her put dishes on the table or collecting silverware. Small things that showed a level of comfort she had only dreamed of until recently. She tried not to feel jealous of Ryan and Sara being together when she couldn't be with Basir, but it was a challenge. If Colonel Spencer hadn't shown up, she would be at the park with Basir, enjoying their second date.

The conversation stayed light over dinner, and Meghan's mood lifted. Despite her doubts and worry about intruding, she had to admit Sara had done her a favor by inviting her to dinner. The companionship of one of the most important people in her life and the woman who was important to him helped her relax and believe everything would turn out all right. After all, Ryan would be more concerned if Basir had gone somewhere dangerous. Wouldn't he?

Memories floated through her mind of all the nonchalant and lighthearted letters and conversations when he was in Afghanistan. He had been in danger then, yet he had purposely avoided telling her anything that would make her worry about him. Was his seeming lack of concern about Basir's current location an act?

As she tried to figure out a way to ask without making him mad, Sara spoke. "So, Ryan, Meghan told me she has no idea where Basir's gone."

"That's right." He finished off the last bit of his meal and leaned back in his chair with a contented smile. "Delicious as usual, Sara."

"Thank you." She glanced at Meghan, her expression showing she saw right through the attempt at changing the subject. "Do you know where Basir went or when he'll be back?"

"I can't say." Tension stiffened Ryan's posture ever so slightly, despite his attempt to appear relaxed.

"Even though you're his roommate and best friend?" Sara rolled her eyes. "Come on, Ryan. I find it hard to believe you know nothing about his sudden disappearance."

"I didn't say that." He pushed his plate aside and crossed his arms on the edge of the table. "I said I can't tell you anything. He went with Colonel Spencer, as Meghan already knows, but that's all I can tell you."

Meghan couldn't leave Sara alone in this quest for information. "Do you know more than that?"

Ryan closed his eyes and sucked in a deep breath. As he slowly released it, he locked his gaze onto her. "Yes, but I can't tell you what."

"Why can't you tell her?" Sara asked. "I mean, he's going out with her, and you're her brother. Can't you at least give her some idea of when he'll be back?"

"No!" Ryan shoved his chair back and stood. He paced across the kitchen and back. Meghan wondered if Sara had made a mistake by pushing him. Then he stopped at the end of the table with a pained expression. "I wish I could tell you what's going on, where Basir is, and when he'll be back. But I can't. Colonel Spencer swore me to secrecy, and I will not break my word to him. I'm sorry, but that's the way it is."

Meghan's fear of Basir going back to Afghanistan renewed, she fought to stay calm. "I understand, but I need to know something."

"I can't tell you anything."

"I just need to know if he's safe wherever the colonel took him." She looked her brother in the eye and prayed he would be willing to give her the reassurance she craved. "And I need to know if he really is coming back. Can you at least tell me that much?"

Ryan rounded the table and knelt beside her. "Megs, I already told you Colonel Spencer will bring him back soon. I can't tell you when that will be, but it shouldn't be too long."

"Is he safe?" Tears burned her eyes, but she blinked them away. She had already cried too much.

"Yes, he is." Ryan laid a hand on her shoulder. "Why would you think he isn't?"

"When marines show up and suddenly take away one of their former interpreters, it's a little suspicious. Especially when it's all such a big secret that no one can even tell me, the woman he's dating, what's going on."

"Ah, Megs." Ryan wrapped her in a hug. "Basir is fine and perfectly safe. I know it's hard not knowing any details, but you're just going to have to trust me on this one."

"I'll try." She took a calming breath as he returned to his seat. Somehow, she would just have to survive in ignorance and hope it didn't drive her completely crazy before Basir showed up again.

~*~

The next few days were an exercise in determination. In a way, the whole situation felt surreal, almost as if Ryan and Basir had never lived in her house. Once again, Meghan was responsible for everything from caring for the alpacas to weeding to her yarn business. Ryan's work schedule kept him too busy to stop by and help out, but she didn't mind too much. The time alone gave her plenty of opportunity to take her worries to God and seek His comfort and guidance.

Yet she couldn't seem to ease the building stress. Until Ryan and Basir started helping her around the farm, she never realized just how much responsibility she had shouldered. Now that she was on her own again, the weight of it pressed down, threatening to crush her at any moment. She would survive and eventually get used to doing it all herself again, but she didn't want to. No matter how selfish it might be, she wanted Basir back. Wanted him puttering around the farm doing whatever work presented itself. Wanted him to show up in the kitchen at mealtime and sit at the table with her.

She wanted him to give her a hug and assure her he would never disappear without a word again.

The alpacas milled around their pens, waiting for their breakfast. Meghan filled a pair of buckets with feed and carried them to the first pen. After filling the trough, she went back to the feed room for the next round. As she headed for the second pen, one of the bucket handles broke, sending feed scattering across the barn aisle.

Meghan stared at the mess, and something deep inside snapped. She sank to the cool concrete as tears rolled down her cheeks. How had she ever survived on her own? How much longer could she possibly be expected to keep going without any word from Basir?

"Oh, God, please give me strength," she whispered in the early morning silence. "Mine is completely tapped."

No sudden burst of energy filled her. The tears

didn't miraculously stop, yet somehow God had heard her. He would help her do everything she needed to do. Right at that moment, what she needed more than anything was a good cry to release all the tension, worry, and fear that had been building since Colonel Spencer showed up on her farm.

Prayers rolled from her heart, laying everything at God's feet, as the tears streamed from her eyes. With each passing moment, the weight lifted from her. She would survive, even thrive, regardless of whether she had human assistance or not. She had God by her side, and with Him as her partner and leader in life, everything would work out. After all, even Romans chapter eight, verse twenty-eight said, "And we know that all things work together for good to them that love God, to them who are the called according to His purpose."

Finally, she dried her eyes and took a shaky breath. If she had known how much better she would feel after crying, she wouldn't have fought so hard against it for so long. She reached for the broken bucket, but the sound of footsteps at the barn entrance caught her attention.

"Meghan?" Basir's deep voice brought fresh tears to her eyes, and she looked over as he dropped a knapsack on the ground and hurried toward her. He knelt before her and searched her face. "Are you all right? What happened?"

She could hardly think of anything to say with her heart so filled with joy at the sight of him. "The handle broke, and I've been so worried about you, and...I'm so glad you're back!"

She rose up on her knees and threw her arms around his neck. He held her close and rubbed her back as he spoke softly.

"I missed you too. I am sorry I had to leave so suddenly and couldn't tell you."

"You're here now. That's the important thing." She relished the feel of his embrace and said a silent prayer of thanks he had returned unharmed. "Can you tell me where you went? Ryan said Colonel Spencer swore him to secrecy."

"He did. He warned me not to say anything, either." Basir rocked back on his heels and smoothed her hair away from her face. "But I don't want to lie to you or keep secrets from you. I love you, and you deserve to know the truth."

As much as she wanted to know where he had been, she couldn't let him risk a reprimand. "Basir, I don't want you break your word to Colonel Spencer just for me. It will be difficult not knowing where you were, but I don't want you to risk getting in trouble."

He smiled, a beautiful sight after the last few days. "I made no promise to Colonel Spencer. He said I shouldn't say anything, but he never asked me to promise I wouldn't."

"So, you wouldn't be breaking your word?" Although she felt as if they were creating a loophole in the situation's confidentiality, she wasn't going to argue if he wanted to enlighten her about his activities of the past few days.

"That is right. I will not tell anyone other than you, but I want to tell you. You deserve to know." He took her hand in both of his and looked her in the eye. "Colonel Spencer needed me to act as interpreter for a man in the United States for surgery. The original interpreter got sick, and because of the sensitivity of the situation, the colonel wanted someone he knew he could trust until the other interpreter recovered and could resume his job."

Meghan searched his features but saw no sign of anything but complete sincerity. "I don't understand. Why is a man in need of surgery such a secret?"

"Because of who the man is. It is best if very few people know he is in the country." Basir lowered his gaze. "I cannot tell you his identity. It is too sensitive."

"That's OK." She lifted her free hand and laid it along his jaw. His sharp intake of breath and the sudden warmth in his gaze soothed away her remaining stress. "I'm glad you told me as much as you did. I've been coming up with all kinds of terrible possibilities for where you had gone, and the worst of them left me afraid you wouldn't come back. It hurt deeply to think of losing you."

"You will not lose me." He released her hand and grasped her shoulders. "I love you, Meghan. I will never abandon you."

"I know, but there's always the possibility Colonel Spencer or someone else will need you again."

"This is true, but I will make it clear that you are to know where I go and when I will return." He drew her closer. "I know this may not be the best time or even the right way to do it, but I can't keep silent any longer."

Her heart thundered in her chest. She sensed something big was about to happen, but she couldn't tell from his serious expression whether it was good or not.

He stroked his fingers along her cheek. "Meghan, I want to share the rest of my life with you, and I hope you want to do the same. Will you marry me and become my wife?"

The simple, plain-spoken proposal in one of the least romantic places she could imagine was the most romantic moment in her life. Her heart overflowed, and she blinked back the moisture that sprang to her eyes.

"Yes, Basir, I will marry you. I would love to be your wife."

He gathered her in his arms and held her close. Then he leaned back just far enough to look into her eyes. "You have made me a very happy man."

She started to tell him he had made her happy by proposing, but his lips meeting hers in the gentlest of kisses rendered her speechless. So much emotion came through his kiss, and she clung to him, absorbing every bit of it and reciprocating with her own heightened emotions. He held her tighter, and she never wanted him to let her go.

Unhappy animal sounds came from the pens, and Basir broke the kiss. "It sounds like the alpacas want their breakfast."

Meghan laughed, both relieved and disappointed when he released her. The emotion flowing between them was so strong it nearly overwhelmed her, but she wouldn't have it any other way. She loved Basir, loved the way he had finally opened up to her and let her into his heart. More than anything, she wanted to continue deepening that connection, but the herd was hungry. Animals came first on the farm. The relationship would have to wait a little while longer.

Basir stood and helped Meghan to her feet. "Do you want me to feed the alpacas or clean this up?"

She looked at the spilled feed surrounding them and considered the choices. "I'll feed the herd."

As she filled another bucket and carried it to the

waiting pen, she stole glances at Basir. Seeing him in her barn again was like seeing a finished puzzle. The picture was beautiful, and she had never felt more complete than knowing such an amazing man would be her husband.

Once they had the alpacas happily eating, Meghan and Basir headed up to the house, pausing only long enough to pick up his pack. As they walked, she slipped her hand into his and met his smile with one of her own.

"How did you get here so early?"

"I had them drop me off here instead of the apartment." He gave her hand a gentle squeeze. "I didn't want to wait to see you."

"I'm glad you came straight here, although I kind of wish you hadn't seen me lose it in the barn."

"You never did fully explain that." He stopped her by the garden. "You seemed more upset than a broken bucket handle or spilled feed called for."

"I was. The broken handle was the last straw, so to speak." She remembered the last few days and sighed. "It's been hard since Ryan told me you packed a bag and left. I didn't realize how much I had come to rely on you until you weren't here. Then there was the added stress of worrying about you."

"God is always in control, even when we don't know what is going on."

"I know, and I've been trying to leave all that worry at His feet, but I couldn't seem to let it go. Until this morning, that is. When you got here, I had just finished a long conversation with God and managed to release all the stress and worry that had been building since Friday."

Basir smiled and rubbed his thumb across her

knuckles. "I am glad you turned to God. He is the One who has kept me going no matter how bad things got. He is always faithful, even when our faith wavers."

"He is my Rock." She laid her head on his shoulder. "But I like having you as my other rock."

"I have never been called a rock before, but coming from you it is a great compliment." Basir put his arm around her shoulders as they continued on to the house. "You know, now that we are engaged, I must speak with your father. I need to know he approves of me for you."

"I have no doubt he will approve."

"Even so..."

They arrived at the back door, and Basir opened it. Meghan paused before stepping through. "You can talk to my dad next week. He and my mom are coming down for the town fair and will be here for a few days."

Basir released a breath and smiled. "Good. I will talk to him then. I was a little afraid I would have to talk to him over the phone, but this is a conversation that should happen face to face."

"They'll be here sometime on Monday, and you'll have until they leave Saturday morning to talk to him." Meghan entered the house and turned around to watch Basir follow her. "I'll even be nice and keep my mom out of the way so you guys can talk privately, if you want."

"Thank you." He planted a kiss on her cheek and continued into the kitchen.

Meghan followed him and prayed the conversation with her father would go as well as she hoped. If it didn't, she wasn't sure Basir would still be willing to marry her.

18

"Great. We'll see you in a few minutes." Meghan ended the call with her mother and turned to find Basir and Ryan watching her from their seats at the kitchen table. "Mom and Dad are passing through town now. They'll be here in less than ten minutes."

A flutter of nerves attacked, killing her appetite. She scraped the last of her lunch into the trash and set the plate in the sink. Ryan carried his empty plate over and added it to hers.

"You did tell them you're engaged, right?" he asked as Basir approached with his dishes.

"Yes, and they're excited about it." She looked at Basir. "I can't wait for you to meet them, but I'm still nervous."

He set his dishes on the counter and took her hand. "I am nervous too, but we will both live."

"I know." She moved to his side and leaned against him, thankful he put his arm around her. After waiting so long for him to show affection in some way, having him hold her was even more comforting and amazing than she had imagined. "Once they're here and they meet you, I'll be fine. It's just the waiting that's getting to me."

Ryan grinned and leaned against the counter. "You guys know I'll back you up. There's nothing to worry about."

"You're wrong. There's plenty to worry about, but

very little of it comes anywhere close to realistic." Meghan sighed and straightened. "I need to get these dishes washed, or Mom will insist on doing them the moment she walks in here."

As she washed the few lunch dishes, Basir picked up a dish towel and dried them. Ryan put them away, and soon the kitchen was clean. The sound of a vehicle on the drive set Meghan's pulse racing. Kadwaal roused from his nap by the wall and stood. The kitten's ears twitched, and he yawned as he stretched.

"Sounds like they're here," Ryan said as he headed for the hallway. "I'll go let them in."

Meghan prayed for the strength to survive introducing her fiancé to her parents. Another prayer left her heart that they would all like each other.

"It will be fine." Basir took her hand and led her toward the hall. "If anyone needs to worry, it is me, not you. They are your parents. I am some stranger who plans to marry their only daughter."

"Like Ryan said, there's nothing to worry about. I'm sure they'll love you."

"I hope so, because I love you." Basir stopped her and gave her a quick kiss. Then he studied her with uncertain eyes. "Will they mind if I hold your hand or put my arm around you like I do in front of Ryan?"

"They won't mind. In fact, they might get suspicious if you don't do stuff like that." Meghan gave him a hug and then led him by the hand to the front door. "Any way that you show affection will only prove to them that you really do love me."

She opened the door, but Basir tugged on her hand to prevent them from going outside. Glancing back, she found him looking at the floor.

"What's wrong?"

"The sun...I need my sunglasses if I want to avoid pain." He shook his head and sighed. "I wish I didn't need them, but I already have a bit of a headache. I don't want to trigger a migraine."

"Oh, I'm sorry, Basir. I didn't think." She looked outside. Her parents were approaching with Ryan between them. "We'll wait here for them and introduce you inside."

"Thank you." His right hand went over his heart in a gesture she had seen less frequently since he returned from his trip.

She gave his arm a quick rub and turned to greet her parents. "Hey, I'm glad you made it."

"You know we can't miss the fair," Dad said as he wrapped her in a bear hug reminiscent of the ones her brother gave.

Mom stepped forward to take her turn. "Especially when our little girl is newly engaged."

Meghan hugged her mother tightly, relieved to see big parental smiles. Then she stepped back and grasped Basir's hand, tugging him to her side. "I guess I should introduce you to your future son-in-law. Basir Hamidi, these are my parents, Fred and Linda Carpenter."

Basir covered his heart and bowed his head. "It is an honor to meet you both."

Dad chuckled and looked at Meghan. "I like this one. Very respectful."

"Yes, he is." She met Basir's gaze and gave his hand a squeeze before focusing on her parents again. "I'm glad you approve."

"Well..." Dad's expression turned serious, and he stroked his chin. "I can't say for sure if I approve completely. After all, I just met the man."

Meghan felt Basir's tension and opened her mouth, but her mother beat her to it.

"Fred!" Mom rolled her eyes and smiled at Basir. "Don't worry, honey. He approves of you. He just thinks he's being funny."

"Linda, you're giving away my secrets." He shook his head and sighed, a gesture that would have been more convincing without the teasing twinkle in his eyes. "She's right, though. Ryan's told us about you, and from what he says, you're perfect for our daughter and will treat her right."

"Yes, I will." A mew at Basir's feet interrupted the conversation, and he reached down to scoop up his kitten. He straightened and smiled. "This is Kadwaal. He likes to be involved in whatever is going on."

"Just like a child." Mom reached out and petted the kitten's head. "He's adorable."

"Thank you."

Meghan suddenly realized they were still crowded by the door, and heat crept into her cheeks. When had she forgotten how to be a good hostess? "Why don't we go sit down to talk? Or you guys can get settled in the guest room. Whatever you want."

"Why don't we talk for a while?" Mom said. "I want to hear about how you and Basir met, how he proposed, and everything else."

Meghan's heart lifted as she ushered them into the living room. Every worry she'd harbored that her parents wouldn't approve of her choice for a husband melted away, and she sent a smile toward Ryan. Thanks to him telling Mom and Dad about Basir, he had smoothed the way for the coming conversation. Basir would have an easier time as well, since the man who knew him better than anyone had vouched for him and clearly given a good report.

As she sat beside Basir on the sofa, she sent a prayer of thanks heavenward.

~*~

Basir watched clouds approach and prayed they would cover the sun. Then he could remove his dark glasses and not have to worry about searing pain. As it was, he kept them on and returned his focus to the conversation around him. Meghan had brought her parents out to see the fruits of her labor, and he and Ryan had tagged along. After touring the vegetable garden and the herb garden, they had ended up by the alpacas lazing the afternoon away in the pasture.

"Your farm is thriving," Fred told his daughter with a proud smile on his face.

"The yarn business is doing well too," Meghan said. "In fact, I'm thinking about expanding the herd in order to keep up with the demand."

"That's a big move. Can your business support the added expense?"

"I've been keeping a careful eye on the books, and I think it can. I'm getting more orders through my website, and I've had a couple of yarn shops express interest in stocking my yarn. At some point, I may raise my prices too. The demand is growing, but I can only produce so much."

Ryan straightened from where he leaned on the fence. "Sounds like you need to consider hiring another spinner to help you out."

Basir considered volunteering, but he wasn't sure if she wanted someone who only knew how to use a drop spindle.

"Maybe." Meghan studied her brother with a teasing twinkle in her eyes. "Want to moonlight on the weekends?"

He laughed and shook his head. "Sorry, sis. I have enough to keep me busy right now. Speaking of which, I need to go pick up Sara."

"Why? Can't wait to introduce her to Mom and Dad?"

"That too, but mainly it's getting close to time for your alpaca walking lesson." Ryan studied her. "You do remember that your helpers are coming this afternoon to learn what to do during the parade, right?"

She closed her eyes and groaned, an action Basir found positively adorable. His fiancée was such an expressive woman, so different from what he had known before. He wasn't sure how he could ever have been attracted to anyone less vibrant, less compassionate.

"I completely forgot they were coming!" Meghan blew out a breath and glanced at her watch. "I better get the alpacas inside and haltered."

"I gotta go," Ryan said and headed in the general direction of the house. "See you soon!"

Meghan looked at her parents. "Sorry to cut the tour short, but I have four kids and Ryan's girlfriend coming in just a little bit and the alpacas they need are out there with the rest of the herd."

"No, they aren't." Basir smiled when she turned a questioning gaze on him. "I put them in the barn before lunch so they would be easy to find."

"You have just saved my sanity." She moved to his side and kissed his cheek. "Thank you."

"You're welcome." He hesitated but then risked

her parents' wrath and put his arm around her. Fred and Linda both smiled, and he relaxed. "Why don't I put the halters on them? I am sure you would like more time to talk to your parents."

"I would, but I don't want to make you do all the work. Especially since I'm the one who forgot everyone was coming." She bit her lip and shifted her gaze between him and her parents.

His heart melted, and he gave her a one-armed hug. "I don't mind the work."

"I know, but..." She sighed and looked at her parents. "Do you guys mind if I leave you on your own for a little while?"

"That's fine, sweetheart," Fred said with a smile. "Don't let us get in the way of your plans."

Linda smiled as well. "Actually, do you mind if I come with you? I'm dying to pet one of those cute little critters of yours."

Basir felt the tension drain out of Meghan, and she nodded. "Sure, you can come meet my parade walkers."

They went to the barn, and Basir collected the harnesses from the wall of the feed room. As he and Meghan haltered the six alpacas and picked pieces of debris from their coats, Fred and Linda asked a few questions and petted the friendly animals. Soon the alpacas were ready and waiting in their pen.

Tires crunched on the gravel drive, and Basir stepped to the open barn door. Ryan parked near the back of the house, and then he and Sara stepped out. Basir waved to them before turning to the others.

"Ryan is back with Sara."

Linda's face lit up. "Oh, good! I want to meet the young lady who has captured my son's attention."

Meghan ushered her parents outside, but Basir didn't immediately follow. He stepped into the feed room and retrieved a small box from a high shelf. Thankfully, Meghan rarely entered the feed room these days. It made the perfect hiding place.

He lifted out his special project and returned the box to the shelf. The ring he had made from scraps of copper wire and solder gleamed dully in the light, and he checked once more to make sure there were no rough spots. He had no idea what an engagement ring looked like, hadn't even known one was expected until Ryan told him a few days ago, but he had done his best to make something beautiful for his bride-to-be. The delicate copper wires were twisted and braided in an intricate design vaguely reminiscent of a ring he had once seen in an advertisement. Tiny beads of solder added a touch of silver here and there while also holding the ring together. He hoped Meghan liked it, because he wasn't sure he could make anything nicer. Buying a ring was out, especially if he wanted to be able to afford a wedding ring for her.

Sunglasses on, he stepped outside and found Sara receiving the same warm greeting from Meghan and Ryan's parents that he had. His heart filled with the knowledge that he was accepted as much as she was, and the naysaying voices in the back of his mind faded a little more.

Basir stopped beside Ryan, who hung back a little. Nerves attacked, but he held out the ring anyway. "What do you think?"

Ryan took it and turned it in his fingers. "You made this?"

"Yes."

"That's amazing." Ryan returned the ring and

grinned. "I assume it's for Meghan."

"Of course. Do you think she will like it?"

"She'll love it." Ryan looked toward his girlfriend and lowered his voice a little. "Do you think you could make another one?"

"Yes, but it won't be identical to this one." That design was for Meghan only.

"That's fine. Any design you think a woman would like will work." Ryan glanced at Basir. "Don't tell anyone, but I'm going to ask Sara to marry me."

"Your secret is safe." Basir laid a hand on his friend's shoulder. "Give me a few days, and I will have a ring for you."

"Thanks, man."

Ryan rejoined his girlfriend, and Meghan walked over to Basir. "You guys looked like you were having a pretty intense conversation."

"We were discussing this." He opened his hand to reveal the ring lying on his palm.

She gasped and touched it with a fingertip. "It's beautiful! Did you make it?"

"Yes." He picked it up and held it out. "It is for you."

Her eyes flooded, and he worried he had made a serious mistake. Then she took the ring and slipped it on the fourth finger of her left hand. It fit perfectly, and he thanked his memories of holding her hand for helping him get the size right.

She threw her arms around him and held him tightly. "I love it. Thank you."

Uncomfortably aware of the others watching, he slid his arms around her and hugged her close. "You're welcome."

After a moment, she stepped back and dried her

eyes. Then she grabbed his hand and pulled him toward the others. As she showed off her homemade engagement ring, he caught the approving glances her parents exchanged. Hope sprang to life deep within him. Maybe asking for her father's permission to marry her wouldn't be so difficult after all.

19

Basir waved to the crowd as the Marine Corps float slowly rolled down the street. Wearing the tan T-shirt, camouflage pants, and boots felt strange, almost as if he had stepped back into his role as interpreter. But Ryan and another man wore similar uniforms, and the others on the float either wore Marine Corps T-shirts or the dress uniform. It was a strange mix in a strange environment. Never would he have expected to be in a parade with people cheering as he passed.

He turned to Ryan, who stood next to him. "I still don't understand how I am on this thing with you."

"Around here, you count as an honorary marine. After all, you worked with us and helped us out with our missions." Ryan patted him on the back and grinned. "All marines, honorary or otherwise, get a spot on the float for the parade."

Basir shook his head and waved at a young family. At least the day had turned cloudy, making his sunglasses and hat unnecessary. From the look of the sky, they might soon need umbrellas. That didn't deter people from lining the streets to watch the floats, high school marching band, tractors, Boy Scouts, and numerous other parade entries pass by. Somewhere ahead of the flatbed trailer Basir rode on, Meghan, Sara, and four children from church walked half-a-dozen alpacas. He wished he were with them, but he was proud to be a part of the parade at all. Before coming to America, he would have suffered disdain rather than appreciation.

The float stopped, bringing his thoughts to a halt as well. He glanced at Ryan. "Why are we stopping?"

"Don't know." He looked ahead and tensed. "Uh-oh."

Before Basir could ask what was wrong, an alpaca trotted past trailing its lead rope. Adrenaline surged through his veins as he met Ryan's gaze.

"I'll catch it," Ryan said, already heading for the side of the float. "You go check on Meghan and the others."

As soon as his boots touched the pavement, Basir took off down the street. After passing several parade entries, he reached Meghan's group. She had her arm around a tearful little girl who was only about eight or nine years old. Neither one appeared injured, and the rest of the people and alpacas appeared unharmed as well. Some of Basir's apprehension faded, and he slowed his steps as he approached them.

"What happened?" he asked as he reached Meghan.

"Jenny's alpaca spooked and yanked the rope out of her hands." She turned a worried gaze on him. "Did you happen to see him?"

"Yes, Ryan is catching him now."

"Good."

Jenny looked up at her. "I'm really sorry, Miss Meghan. I tried to hold on to him, but he was too strong."

"I know, honey. It's OK." She gave the girl a hug and met Basir's gaze. "Basir, once Ryan brings Chewy back, would you mind taking over walking him? I don't trust him to behave at this point."

"Of course."

Ryan showed up a moment later with a placid alpaca at his side. "Lose someone, sis?"

She rolled her eyes as Basir took the rope. "Nope. He just decided to go for a little walk without human supervision."

"That misbehaving critter." Ryan heaved a sigh and shook his head, and then he knelt beside the still upset girl. "Hey, Jenny, what's wrong?"

"Chewy escaped from me." She sniffled and hiccupped. "He got scared by something, and I couldn't hold onto him."

"Well, no harm done. I'm sure you did the best you could, and that's the important thing." He offered her a smile then stood and looked at his sister. "I assume Basir's taking over with Chewy?"

"Right. I don't trust him not to spook again before the end of the route."

"In that case..." He focused on Jenny again. "Since Basir is taking your place here, how would you like to take his place with me?"

"Really? I can ride with the marines?" She looked up at Meghan with wide eyes and an awed expression. "Is that OK, Miss Meghan?"

"Sure. We can explain what happened to your parents later." She gave the girl one more hug. "You have fun with Ryan."

"I will!"

Ryan held out his hand, and Jenny took it with a big grin on her face. She skipped along beside him back toward the Marine Corps float, and Basir chuckled as he took his place beside Meghan.

"She cheered up quickly."

Meghan laughed as they started walking. "I think

she has a bit of a crush on Ryan. She's always so excited when he helps out with junior church."

"Sara will be so jealous."

The woman in question glanced back from her place several feet ahead. "Why will I be jealous?"

Meghan laughed again, the sound like music in the muggy air. "Because Jenny's riding with Ryan instead of you."

"That's no reason to be jealous." Sara grinned. "He'll just have to make it up to me later."

Basir chuckled and enjoyed the laughter of the kids around them. Despite the vague sense of danger from being so exposed and surrounded by crowds, he was enjoying himself. He had come so far in the time he'd known Meghan, and the best part of it was that he was no longer afraid to love her. No, he wasn't the same man he had been before working with the marines and getting injured, but he was no less of a man now. His honor was no longer in question.

During his time working as a temporary interpreter, he'd had a chance to talk to Colonel Spencer about everything going on in his life. The colonel had been happy to hear about his relationship with Meghan and had offered a few pieces of advice. The most important advice he had given Basir involved cutting ties with the past and embracing the future. Yes, he had a lifetime of memories and trauma to work through and live with, but he also had a woman who loved him and wanted to see him happy. As Colonel Spencer had said, the love of a good woman could get a man through just about anything. The closer Basir drew to Meghan, the more he saw the truth of that statement.

The one thing Meghan's love couldn't do,

however, was cure his brain. As they walked toward the town's park, where the parade ended and the fair waited, Basir felt the telltale twinges of pain in his skull that signaled worse to come. He could only pray he would get back to the apartment and take his medication in time to keep it from becoming excruciating.

~*~

"You did a great job with Luna," Meghan said as she accepted the lead rope from eleven-year-old Peter. The black alpaca nuzzled his arm before moving to Meghan's side. "I think you have a new friend."

"She's really nice." He petted the alpaca one more time and stepped back. "See you at church."

He trotted off to join his parents nearby, and Meghan tied the rope to the side of the trailer. Only two more alpacas to retrieve, one from a kid and one from Sara, and then she and Basir could load them up and take them back to the farm. Ten-year-old Ashley handed her alpaca's lead rope to Basir and ran off to join her family before Meghan could thank her. A smile formed as she watched the girl's animated gestures while talking to her parents. Ashley was such an awkward child that it warmed Meghan's heart to see her so excited and lively.

She turned to say as much to Basir, but the words caught in her throat as he stumbled and braced a hand on the alpaca's shoulder. He closed his eyes and took slow, deep breaths, swaying slightly.

Meghan hurried to his side and laid a hand on his back. "What's wrong?"

"Dizzy." He opened his eyes and slowly turned

his pale face toward her. "I don't feel well."

"Are you sick?" She searched his face, seeing only strained features.

"Not yet." He sucked in another breath and slowly released it. "Bad migraine."

"I'm sorry." She gave his back a sympathetic rub. "Why don't you hand me Riki's lead so I can tie her to the trailer? Then, I'll help you sit down so you don't fall over."

"OK." He handed her the rope and stayed still as she led the alpaca to the side of the trailer and secured her.

When she returned to his side, he draped an arm over her shoulders as she slipped an arm around his waist. Sara joined them before they took a single step.

"Is everything OK?"

"Not exactly." Meghan bit her lip and thought fast. "Can you find Ryan and tell him Basir needs to go home?"

"Sure. No problem. I'll go as soon as I tie this guy with the others."

"Thanks, Sara." Meghan focused on Basir, who leaned heavily against her. "Come on. You can sit in my truck until Ryan shows up."

He didn't respond, but she didn't really expect him to. Pain showed clearly on his face, and she prayed his suffering wouldn't last too long or get any worse. It worried her how quickly the migraine had hit, however. He had seemed fine during the parade, maybe a little quiet toward the end, but that wasn't unusual for him. Normally his migraines seemed to either come with warning signs like a worsening headache or be triggered by something, such as a bright light. This one appeared to have hit without warning.

She helped him onto the passenger seat, and he leaned his head against the doorframe as he looked at her through sad tawny-brown eyes. A lock of dark hair fell over his forehead, and she brushed it back.

"How are you doing?" She kept her voice soft, knowing noise could make some migraines worse.

"Not good." He sighed and lifted a hand to touch her cheek. "Are you sure you want to marry a man with debilitating headaches?"

"Yes." She grasped his hand and placed a gentle kiss on his fingers. "I love you, Basir, and I agreed to marry you in spite of the permanent injuries you have. Remember?"

"I remember, but..." He lowered his gaze. "I can't think positively right now."

"That's all right. I'll think positively for both of us."

A faint smile touched his lips, and he met her gaze again. "You are good for me, *zerrgay*."

"You're good for me too." She gave his hand a gentle squeeze. "But what does that word mean?"

"Which word?"

"The last one. Zer-something."

He studied her for a moment, and then his expression cleared. "*Zerrgay*. It means, um...I can't think of the English word right now. But it means I care about you and you are important to me."

"Oh." From his description, it sounded as if the word was a term of endearment, similar to *sweetheart* or *darling*. Regardless of the literal translation, the emotion behind it was all that truly mattered.

He closed his eyes with a sigh, and Meghan turned to scan the crowd. She didn't see any sign of her brother. Hopefully, Sara would find him soon. Basir clearly needed to lie down, and the sooner the better.

She heard movement behind her and glanced back to see Basir looking a little green. Before she could say anything, he bolted from the truck and headed for the row of portable toilets across the parking lot. He disappeared into one, and Meghan prayed he was all right.

"Hey, Megs!" Ryan's voice behind her drew her attention, and she turned around to find him approaching with their parents and Sara trailing behind. "Where's Basir?"

She waved a hand at the blue plastic stalls. "He's in the end one. He didn't look too good."

"Aw, man." Ryan jammed his fingers into his hair. "Another migraine?"

"Yeah, and it looks like a bad one."

"All right." He blew out a breath and turned to Sara, who now stood beside him. "Do you mind hanging out with my sister for a little while? I'll come back and pick you up after I get Basir settled at home."

"That's fine. I'll just help her load up the alpacas or something." Sara kissed his cheek, and then he followed the same path Basir had taken only moments before.

Meghan longed to go with him to make sure Basir was all right, but she had a feeling staying out of the way was a better idea. She shifted her attention to her parents, who had joined her with confused expressions.

"Meghan, what is going on?" Dad asked.

"Basir gets these migraines sometimes..." She wasn't sure how much to say, but she couldn't lie to her parents. "One hit, and he needs to go home and lie down. Since I have the alpacas with me, it'll be easier for Ryan to take him."

"Poor guy," Mom said, her expression full of sympathy. "Does he get them often?"

"Often enough." Meghan looked across the parking lot in time to see Ryan helping Basir along. "Sometimes they're worse than others."

Dad turned from watching the two men, his gaze suspicious. "He looks drunk."

"He's not. He doesn't drink alcohol, ever. The migraines sometimes make him dizzy."

"I see." Dad glanced at Mom. "Let's go explore the fair a little more, Linda."

"All right." She gave Meghan a warm smile and a pat on the arm. "We'll see you back at your house."

"Have fun." Meghan prayed her father wouldn't change his mind about Basir because of a medical condition. Without Dad's approval, her relationship with Basir would never go anywhere. He was so intent on doing everything the right way that he wouldn't dare marry her without her father's blessing.

20

A soft paw poked Basir's chin, and he struggled to open his eyes. A faint glow seeped around the heavy curtain over the window, providing a hint of illumination in the otherwise dark bedroom. Kadwaal leaned over him and looked him in the eye.

"*Mrrow*?"

Basir smiled and lifted a hand to stroke the kitten. As he slowly grew more alert, he realized that all traces of nausea and dizziness were finally gone. His head still ached a little, but nowhere near as badly as the previous evening. He could survive the dull ache throbbing in his skull.

The kitten pawed at him again, and he realized someone was moving around the kitchen. There wasn't nearly as much banging as when Ryan cooked, but there was enough noise to make it clear someone was working in there. Basir looked toward the alarm clock on the dresser. The glowing red numbers showed it was the middle of the afternoon. He had slept for nearly twenty hours, with only a few brief interruptions.

He sat up with a groan and scrubbed a hand across his face. Stubble rasped against his palm, and he glanced at the kitten watching him intently. "I hope Fred Carpenter doesn't think I am too weak to marry his daughter."

As soon as he spoke the words, he wanted to lie

down and go back to sleep. Possibly forever. How could he ever hope to win the man's approval when he hadn't even been able to work on Meghan's farm that morning? What did he have to prove he could provide for her? He didn't even have a small home to call his own, let alone a regular job with a reliable income. The only money he earned came from the woman he wanted to marry. Not exactly the best indication that he could take care of her.

Kadwaal climbed in his lap and leaned against him with a purr. The warm, vibrating body helped draw him out of his thoughts, and he released a breath as he stroked the kitten's side.

"I know, little one. You think I am the greatest thing since food."

Kadwaal meowed and jumped down. He trotted to the door, which stood open a few inches to allow him to come and go at will. Instead of leaving, he looked over his shoulder and meowed again.

"All right, Kadwaal. I get the message. You are hungry." Basir climbed out of bed and stretched. He was finally hungry too, so he might as well find out who was in his kitchen and get something to eat.

He followed his kitten into the living room and spotted Ryan sprawled on the couch with a book in his hands. A pause in his steps alerted his friend to his presence, and Ryan lowered the book.

"Hey, you're still alive."

Basir managed a smile, despite his increased curiosity about who was cooking. "Yes, I am alive and plan to stay that way for a while."

"Good to know." Ryan lifted his book. "You should let Meghan know, too. She's been worried about you."

His heart lifted with the knowledge the woman he loved had been thinking about him. "I will tell her after I eat something."

"Good luck with that."

Basir sent a questioning look his way, but Ryan ignored him so he continued on to the kitchen. As soon as he stepped into the room, he understood Ryan's comment. Meghan stood at the stove stirring a small, steaming pot. The warm scents of chicken and vegetables filled the air, making his stomach rumble in anticipation. Kadwaal trotted to his food bowl and began crunching on the waiting kibble. So much for his kitten needing him to provide food.

Meghan turned around and studied him with a hopeful gaze. "Hey. How are you feeling?"

"Much better." He joined her by the stove and peered over her shoulder. "What are you cooking?"

"Chicken soup." She turned around, placing her face inches from his. "Ryan said you haven't eaten since sometime yesterday."

"He is right. I have been sleeping." He stepped back, aware his breath could probably kill. Why hadn't Ryan warned him she was here? He would have taken a few moments to clean up before going in search of food.

"All the sleep appears to have done wonders for you." She smiled and waved a hand toward the pot. "Hungry?"

"Very."

"Have a seat, and I'll fill a bowl."

Basir pulled out a chair at the table and dropped into it. He watched her move around his kitchen, appearing as comfortable as she was in her own. Within moments, he had a healthy serving of hearty soup in front of him. Meghan sat down across from him as he said a quick prayer of thanks for his meal.

As he scooped up his first bite of chicken and vegetable-laden broth, he gave her a questioning look. "Should you tell Ryan the soup is ready?"

"Nope." She reached across the table to touch his hand. "I made that for you."

"Thank you." He ate a spoonful to give himself time to recover from his shock. She had come all the way to town just to make him a bowl of soup? If that didn't prove her love for him, he didn't know what would. "This is good."

"Thanks." She watched him eat a few more bites. "My mom wanted me to let you know she and my dad have been praying for a speedy recovery for you."

"That is kind of them. Where are your parents?"

"My mom talked my dad into visiting the antique shop down the street and a couple of other shops she spotted. We'll meet back at the farm for dinner."

Basir nodded and continued eating. If her parents were praying for him, that was a good sign. Right? They wouldn't pray for a man they didn't like. Or would they? He knew many Christians who would pray for their worst enemy. But surely the Carpenters wouldn't have allowed their daughter to come cook for him if they viewed him as an enemy. Perhaps having them find out about one of his weaknesses wouldn't ruin the possibility of a happy future with Meghan after all.

Only one way to find out. He laid his spoon in the bowl and focused on his fiancée. "Would you mind if I went with you to your farm this evening?"

"Of course I don't mind." She tilted her head at an inquisitive angle. "You do realize Ryan and I took care of all the chores, right?"

"I assumed you had done so. I want to go to your farm tonight so that I can speak with your father."

"Are you up to that conversation right now?" A small furrow formed between her eyebrows. "He'll be here until Saturday."

"I need to talk to him as soon as possible." Basir shook his head and sighed. "I know you don't understand, but I need to know I have his permission to marry you. Without that..."

"I know." She reached across the table and grasped his hand. "You can come home with me, and I'll make sure you have a chance to talk to my dad."

"Thank you." His heart thumped with a combination of anticipation and worry. Would Fred grant his blessing, or would he break two hearts?

Ryan stepped into the kitchen. "Hey, I'm going to go. Sara's waiting for me."

"All right." Meghan smiled at her brother. "Be sure to let her know you're both welcome to join us at the farm for dinner."

"I will. See you guys later." He left the room, and a moment later the front door opened and shut.

A wave of nerves washed over Basir, but he continued eating to hide it. He had never been alone in his apartment with Meghan before. Somehow, it felt different than being alone with her at her farm. More intimate and capable of getting them both in trouble. Yet he didn't know what to do about it. He could ask her to leave, but that would be rude. Besides, he needed her to provide transportation to her farm. The only other option that popped into his mind was to get them out of there as quickly as possible.

He finished his soup and carried his bowl to the

sink, planning to wash it later. "I will go change, and then we can leave."

"All right," Meghan said as she slowly rose from her seat. "But there's no rush."

"Meghan, I—" He wasn't sure how to explain his need for either a chaperone or a new location without sounding like a crazy man. "Please?"

She studied him for a moment and then nodded. "OK. I'll clean up the kitchen while you get ready."

"Thank you." He smiled and left the room.

~*~

Basir rushed through a shower and shaving, and then he dressed in fresh jeans and a T-shirt. He wasn't sure what the proper etiquette was for a man talking to a prospective father-in-law in America, but he had a feeling the conversation would go better if he looked respectable. He also had a feeling discussing anything resembling a bride price was out of the question. After talking to Ryan and Colonel Spencer, he knew that Fred's main concerns would likely be whether Basir could take care of his daughter and any children they might someday have and whether he would treat her well.

Treating Meghan well wasn't an issue. He wasn't sure he could ever do anything else. Providing for her needs and the needs of any children, however, was a different story. Since his only means to support anyone came from Meghan herself, he wasn't sure if Fred would consider that enough. But maybe he could convince the man that he would become Meghan's partner in the farm and help ensure it flourished by using his knowledge of farming and raising wool-bearing animals.

Worrying about the coming conversation wouldn't help it go more smoothly. Basir straightened his shoulders and left the hallway with his kitten on his heels. When he stepped into the kitchen, he found Meghan putting the now-clean pan in the cabinet. She closed the door and turned around with a smile.

"Perfect timing. I just finished in here."

Basir glanced at the kitten winding around his ankles. "I need to put Kadwaal's harness on, and then we can go."

He returned to the living room and grabbed the small blue harness and matching leash from the table beside the door. Kadwaal meowed loudly, his purr even louder, when he saw it.

"Come here, little one." Basir knelt and the kitten stood remarkably still as he strapped the harness on. From what he had heard, training a cat to accept a harness and walk on a leash was usually a near-impossible task, but Kadwaal had taken to both easily. He stood, slipped the handle of the leash around his wrist, and looked at Meghan. "Ready?"

"Whenever you are."

Her smile increased his heartrate, and he turned to open the door. The sooner they got out of there, the better. His thoughts were headed down a path they had no business going, especially since he couldn't be certain he would be able to marry her. But even if he were certain they would wed, he had to keep his thoughts toward her completely pure. Anything less would disrespect her.

Once in the hall, he locked the door behind them. Kadwaal trotted happily at his side to the stairs, and Basir paused to scoop up the kitten. His furry friend could go up and down the stairs on his own, but it was a time-consuming task.

Soon they were in Meghan's truck on the way to her farm. Basir stared out the window, his thoughts twisting back and forth between the coming conversation with Fred and the ring he had promised to make for Ryan. By the time they parked at the back of Meghan's house, he had a good idea of the design for the ring, but he still hadn't figured out what to say to Fred. Thankfully, the elder Carpenters' car was absent, so he had a little more time to prepare.

He removed Kadwaal's harness before opening the door. The kitten scrambled to the ground and immediately set off to explore. Basir left the harness and leash on the seat when he climbed out. The kitten still kept close on the farm, so he saw no need to restrain him. During transport from town to farm and back, however, he didn't want to risk the kitten getting too curious about the vehicle and interfering with whoever was driving.

Meghan met Basir by the hood of her truck. "So, what shall we do to entertain ourselves until my parents get here?"

"Well..." He was torn. As much as he wanted to spend time with her just relaxing, he had a promise to keep. "I have project I need to work on for Ryan."

"Can I tag along?" Her sweet smile destroyed any resolve he may have had to keep the ring a secret from her.

"OK, but you can't tell anyone about what I am making."

Meghan laughed as they headed toward the workshop attached to the barn. "That sounds ominous."

"It is not ominous." He grasped her hand and smiled as he felt her ring. "More of a secret for the moment."

"Now I'm even more curious."

He chuckled and let them into the workshop. Meghan flipped the switch by the door, and light flooded the cluttered space. He had organized the tools, materials, and stored items the best he could, but it still looked a little chaotic. The workbench along the back wall was fairly clear, however, and he made his way over to it. A thin strand of insulated wire lay on the wooden surface along with the tools he would need to make a ring. Meghan stood at his side and watched as he picked up the wire and began stripping off the insulation to reveal the copper underneath.

"Will you tell me what you're making?" she asked as he cut the wire into even lengths.

He laid his work down and faced her, amused by the curiosity shining in her eyes. "Do you promise to keep it a secret from Ryan that I let you watch me work?"

"I suppose..." She studied him. "But if you're making it for him, why does it matter if he knows I watched?"

"Because I think he wants to keep it a secret from everyone for now."

"Ah, gotcha. That reminds me of when we were kids around Christmas. We would either make or buy gifts for everyone and try to keep anyone else from knowing what they were until Christmas morning. The whole family enjoyed the surprise of finding out what the gifts were."

Basir wondered what kind of traditions they would share in the coming years, but he pushed the thought aside for the moment. "I am sure your whole family will enjoy this surprise as well."

Meghan bumped her shoulder into his. "The suspense is killing me."

He chuckled and gave her a quick hug. "I am making a ring for your brother."

"A ring? Why would he..." The confusion in her face evaporated as she looked at her left hand. Then her eyes widened and shone with joy. "Oh!"

"Yes. Now you know why it is such a big secret."

"My lips are sealed." She pretended to lock her mouth and toss aside the key.

"This will be a quiet afternoon." Basir picked up the wires and made sure the ends were even as he waited for her reaction to the teasing comment.

She swatted his shoulder. "Oh, please. You know I'm not going to stay silent that long."

"This is true, but I thought it would take a little longer before you started talking again."

She laughed and slid an arm around his waist as she laid her head on his shoulder. "You know, I think it's great you're doing this for him."

"He asked after he saw the ring I made for you." He glanced at her and matched her smile with one of his own. Perhaps one day he would get used to her affectionate ways, but he hoped he never took her affection for granted. He had never experienced anything quite like it, and he never wanted to lose that special connection with her.

He returned his attention to the wire in his fingers, but his mind drifted yet again to what he would say to her father. If he had ever been witness to marriage negotiations, he might have a little more confidence in his ability to say the right things. But he hadn't been regarded highly enough to be party to any such negotiations, and his own marriage had been negotiated without his presence, as was common.

Father God, help me to know what to say when the time comes.

God knew how much he loved Meghan and wanted to marry her. If it was truly in His will for them to be together, they would be, even if Basir completely blew the conversation with Fred. He had to trust that God would help him find the words he needed when he needed them. Otherwise, he was liable to drive himself crazy worrying about it.

21

Meghan scooped a spoonful of cookie dough from the mixing bowl and dropped it on the greased pan. She stole a glance toward the back door, but it still didn't open. After watching Basir manipulate the wires for a while, she had decided to leave him to his work and find something productive to do while she waited for her parents' return. Work held little appeal, so she decided cookies were the answer. Thankfully, she'd gone with a familiar chocolate chip recipe. Trying to focus was an interesting challenge as her mind whirled.

Her brother planned to propose to Sara? It didn't particularly surprise her, but she wanted to wrap them both in a big hug and jump for joy. Then, she had to consider what would happen when Basir talked to her father. Yes, Dad had said a few times how much he liked Basir, but did he like him enough to approve of him as a son-in-law?

At least she knew her mother was thrilled about the engagement. If Dad did anything other than give his blessing for the marriage for some reason, she could count on Mom for backup. She didn't know if that would be enough for Basir, but she had to hope.

"Lord, please let Dad give Basir the permission he needs to marry me. I feel like You brought us together, and if that's the case, I know nothing will keep us from marrying. But I would like everything to be as stress-free and joyful as possible, so please help the conversation between Basir and my dad go smoothly."

She added one last cookie to the pan and slid it into the oven. With that prayer, she had done everything she could to ensure her dad would grant his permission for the wedding. Now she just had to stick to her faith and believe that God would make sure everything worked out the way it was supposed to. Hopefully, that meant she would marry Basir. It had to mean that, because she wasn't sure she could survive the heartache of having him leave her.

The front door opened, and her mother called out, "Hello, hello!"

"I'm in the kitchen!" Meghan set the timer for the cookies and turned to greet her parents.

Mom and Dad stepped into the room with plastic bags in their hands.

"I found the most amazing knickknacks," Mom said as she set two bags on the kitchen table.

Dad added the one he carried. "How's Basir?"

"Doing well." Meghan tried not to read too much into the fact that her father had been the one to ask. "Actually, he's out in the workshop right now."

Dad's eyebrows rose. "He is better."

"Like I said, sleep and his medication usually clear up his migraines in a few hours to a day."

"I'm glad he found something that works," Mom said. "Your Aunt Kathy has had migraines that last for days."

The back door opened and closed, and then Basir stepped into the kitchen. Mom gave him a warm smile.

"Hi, Basir. How are you feeling?"

"Much better. Thank you for your prayers." He bowed his head slightly.

"Oh, you're welcome, honey." Mom walked over and patted his arm. "I'm glad your migraine went away."

"Me too." He glanced at Meghan, and she could see he was ready to talk to her father. Well, maybe not ready, but as close as he was going to get. She had no idea if her parents could sense his nervousness, but she could see it in his eyes and his body language.

She gave him a small nod, and he turned to her father.

"Fred, may I speak with you privately?"

"Of course." Her father looked a little surprised, but he lifted a hand toward the back door. "Why don't we go outside?"

As soon as the men left, Mom turned to Meghan. "That poor young man looks scared half to death."

"He is." She drew in a breath to calm her nerves and decided to let her mom in on the conversation the men were having. "He's going to ask Dad for permission to marry me."

A smile spread across Mom's face. "That's so sweet! A little more old-fashioned than I expected, but it's a nice gesture."

"It's more than a gesture for Basir. He is sincerely seeking Dad's permission to marry me." Meghan shook her head and tried not to worry. "He's done a great job of integrating into American life, but some things he just can't let go. Making sure my father is in agreement over our marriage is one of those things."

Mom stared at her wide-eyed. "You mean he would honestly break off your engagement if your father didn't grant permission for him to marry you?"

"Right. He wants so much to respect and honor me that he would make himself miserable to keep from doing anything that might damage my family's honor...such as marrying me without my father's blessing."

"Well, no wonder he looked so terrified!" Mom moved to Meghan's side and hugged her. "But neither one of you needs to worry. I happen to know your father fully approves of Basir as husband material. In a few minutes, that young man of yours will be able to relax and focus on building his relationship with you."

"Oh, I'm so glad." Meghan sagged in relief, thankful for her mother's support, both physical and moral. Then, she straightened and looked at the bags on her table. "While we wait for them to get back, why don't you show me your new knickknacks?"

As her mom unwrapped the newspaper protecting the first one, Meghan said a silent prayer of thanks that everything would be OK.

~*~

"It's good to see you up and moving around," Fred said as they crossed the back yard. "You didn't look well at all after the parade."

"I wasn't. It was one of the worst migraines I have had in a while." Basir prayed for wisdom as he struggled to know how much to tell the man he hoped would be his father-in-law.

"Have you always had migraines?"

Basir shook his head, thankful for the clouds hiding the sun. At least he didn't have to hide his eyes. "No, the migraines started after the explosion that injured me. The doctors tell me it is part of the traumatic brain injury I suffered."

"That's too bad." Fred glanced at him as they

approached the pasture. "Are the effects of your brain injury serious?"

The moment had come to be completely honest with the man and hope he didn't deem Basir unworthy as a husband. "Serious enough. I have the migraines, and my eyes get more light sensitive. They were already sensitive from the burns. I also get other headaches, dizziness."

"I see." Fred stopped by the fence and turned to face him. "I've heard that traumatic brain injuries can cause personality changes. Is that true for you?"

Basir looked out over the alpacas happily munching on grass as he considered the way he was now compared to how he was before. "I think it has changed me a little, but I don't suffer the uncontrollable anger or impulsiveness of some."

"How has it changed you, then?"

"I am less confident. More anxious." Basir hated admitting such serious weakness before even broaching the topic of marriage, but the man deserved to know the truth. "It is hard for me sometimes to remember that I must live by American standards now and not Afghan standards, but I am getting better. I will never be the man I was before the explosion, but I am improving."

"I'm glad to hear it." Fred leaned against the fence and studied him. "Now, what is it you wanted to talk to me about? I'm sure this isn't it."

"Ah, no." Basir drew in a deep breath and slowly released it. In a few minutes, he would know whether Meghan could become his wife or if he would have to remain alone. "I wanted to talk to you about Meghan. You know I have asked her to marry me. In my homeland, I would not have asked her. I would have talked to my father, and he would have talked to you and arranged the marriage."

"I see." Fred studied him for an uncomfortably long moment. "Since you've already proposed to her, I assume you've figured out our family doesn't do arranged marriages."

"Yes. I understand they are unusual in America."

"So, since you've arranged your own marriage, what is it you wanted to talk to me about?"

"I would like your permission to marry your daughter. I love her with everything that is in me, and I will continue to love her and honor her as long as I live." He held his breath as he waited for Fred's response.

"Can you take care of her? Provide for her and any children the two of you may have?"

"I work hard. I know much about farming and how to make the land productive. Meghan has said that the advice and assistance I have given her have already helped her a great deal. I will continue to do whatever she needs me to do around here to make her farm and Carpenter Alpacas as productive and profitable as possible."

"And you have no problem knowing you'll be working for your wife?"

"No." Basir didn't know how to explain the hard road he had traveled to get to where he was, but complete honesty seemed to be the best option. "I know it may seem odd for me to devote my life to running a farm I do not own, but it is what I know. And Meghan will not fire me when I have bad days. A regular job like Ryan has would not work well for me."

"I see. And Meghan knows all of this? She knows about the traumatic brain injury and the challenges you have because of it?"

"Yes. I have been completely honest with her."

"Good." Fred looked out over the pasture long enough to make Basir worry, but then he brought his gaze back and smiled. "I can tell you love my daughter very much and that she loves you just as much. Do you promise to always treat her with respect and care for her to the best of your ability?"

"Yes." Basir placed his right hand over his heart and prayed the man would see his sincerity. "I would give my life for her if it came to that."

"We'll hope it never comes to that, because it would break my daughter's heart." Fred clapped a hand to Basir's shoulder. "You have my permission to marry Meghan. I appreciate your honesty with me, and I look forward to having you as part of the family."

"Thank you." A weight lifted from Basir, and he said a silent prayer of thanks.

They watched the alpacas while they continued to talk, and Basir answered every question Fred asked about his background and family. Some of it was painful, such as admitting to being disowned, but sharing it all with his future father-in-law was also freeing. Fred never once made him feel ashamed of his past. Instead, he expressed sympathy and compassion just as his children did.

By the time they returned to the house, Basir felt more secure in his relationship with Meghan than he ever had. The women sat at the kitchen table with steaming mugs filling the air with the strong scent of coffee. A plate of chocolate chip cookies waited in the middle of the table.

Meghan ran her gaze over Basir and smiled as her mother rose and followed Fred into the hallway. "You look awful happy."

"Your father has granted his permission for me to marry you." He knelt beside her and took her hand. "He said he looks forward to me being a part of your family."

"That's great news!" She wrapped her arms around his neck and hugged him tight. "No wonder you look so happy."

"Yes. Now nothing stands in the way of our marriage. We are free to wed and start our life together."

"Well, it won't be quite that fast." She leaned back with a small laugh. "My mom is determined to plan the most perfect wedding ever. She thinks a winter wedding is ideal."

"And what do you think?" Winter seemed like a lifetime away, but he would do whatever made Meghan happy. After all, it was her first wedding, and he knew American women wanted their weddings to be perfect.

"I think she's right. It will give us more time to get to know each other, but it's not too far away. What do *you* think?"

"I think..." He leaned closer and smiled as he looked into her eyes. "Whatever will make you happy is what we should do."

Warmth filled her eyes and she opened her mouth, but the sound of the front door interrupted. The murmur of voices reached them, and then Ryan called out, "Hey, Megs! Basir! Come out here."

"Wonder what he wants," Meghan said as they stood.

Basir placed his mouth close to her ear and whispered, "Probably the ring."

She laughed and slipped her hand into his as they stepped into the hall.

Ryan stood just inside the front door with his arm around Sara. Both looked excited, leading Basir to wonder if there was more truth to his teasing comment than he thought. Fred and Linda stood with them, their expressions curious. When Basir and Meghan joined the group, Ryan ran his gaze over each of them.

"Now that you're all here, I have some news. Sara and I are getting married."

"Oh, that's wonderful!" Linda's eyes filled, and she stepped forward to embrace them both.

As congratulations rolled around the group, Ryan met Basir's gaze and mouthed, *Ring?* Basir nodded and stepped to Meghan's side.

"I'll be right back," he said softly.

"OK." She gave him a knowing smile. Then she turned back to the conversation with her mother and Sara.

Basir headed out the back door and hurried to the workshop, thankful he had already finished the ring. The braided piece of jewelry sat on the workbench, and he grabbed it before jogging back to the house. He stepped inside to find the Carpenter family and Sara had moved to the kitchen. Meghan stood at the counter pouring coffee, while her mother set small plates on the table.

Ryan joined Basir near the utility room. "Did you finish it?"

"I made it this afternoon." He handed over the ring.

Ryan studied it and grinned. "This is perfect. Thanks, man."

"You are welcome." Basir's heart filled as he

watched Ryan present the ring to his fiancée. Sara's reaction was similar to Meghan's when she received her ring, and Basir wondered why American women got so emotional over a piece of jewelry. Then, Meghan joined him and slipped her hand into his.

"Isn't it wonderful?" she asked as she leaned lightly against him.

"That they are engaged? Yes." He couldn't be happier for his friend and future brother-in-law.

She looked up at him. "My mom, Sara, and I think a double wedding sometime around Christmas would be awesome."

"What does Ryan think?" Basir had never heard of a double wedding, but if that was what she wanted...

"He thinks it's a great idea too. What do you think?"

"Like I said earlier, we should do whatever makes you happy. As long as you become my wife, the details of the wedding aren't important to me."

"Then we'll plan the double wedding. I can't wait to marry you." She gave him a quick kiss, and then tugged him over to join the group.

As preliminary discussions of the upcoming marriages flew around him, Basir smiled. He had been through war and pain and had hit the lowest point in his life, but God had remained with him through it all and brought him out of that dark pit into an amazing life filled with light and love. In the process, the honor Basir had thought completely destroyed had been redeemed.

He met Meghan's gaze, his heart overflowing. "God is good."

"Yes, He is." She slipped an arm around him, and he knew he had found the place he belonged.

Thank you

We appreciate you reading this White Rose Publishing title. For other inspirational stories, please visit our on-line bookstore at www.pelicanbookgroup.com.

For questions or more information, contact us at customer@pelicanbookgroup.com.

White Rose Publishing
Where Faith is the Cornerstone of Love™
an imprint of Pelican Book Group
www.PelicanBookGroup.com

Connect with Us
www.facebook.com/Pelicanbookgroup
www.twitter.com/pelicanbookgrp

To receive news and specials, subscribe to our bulletin
http://pelink.us/bulletin

May God's glory shine through
this inspirational work of fiction.

AMDG

You Can Help!

At Pelican Book Group it is our mission to entertain readers with fiction that uplifts the Gospel. It is our privilege to spend time with you awhile as you read our stories.

We believe you can help us to bring Christ into the lives of people across the globe. And you don't have to open your wallet or even leave your house!

Here are 3 simple things you can do to help us bring illuminating fiction™ to people everywhere.

1) If you enjoyed this book, write a positive review. Post it at online retailers and websites where readers gather. And share your review with us at reviews@pelicanbookgroup.com (this does give us permission to reprint your review in whole or in part.)

2) If you enjoyed this book, recommend it to a friend in person, at a book club or on social media.

3) If you have suggestions on how we can improve or expand our selection, let us know. We value your opinion. Use the contact form on our web site or e-mail us at customer@pelicanbookgroup.com

God Can Help!

Are you in need? The Almighty can do great things for you. Holy is His Name! He has mercy in every generation. He can lift up the lowly and accomplish all things. Reach out today.

Do not fear: I am with you; do not be anxious: I am your God. I will strengthen you, I will help you, I will uphold you with my victorious right hand.
~Isaiah 41:10 (NAB)

We pray daily, and we especially pray for everyone connected to Pelican Book Group—that includes you! If you have a specific need, we welcome the opportunity to pray for you. Share your needs or praise reports at http://pelink.us/pray4us

Free Book Offer

We're looking for booklovers like you to partner with us! Join our team of influencers today and periodically receive free eBooks!

For more information
Visit http://pelicanbookgroup.com/booklovers

www.ingramcontent.com/pod-product-compliance
Lightning Source LLC
Chambersburg PA
CBHW052044240626
47153CB00006B/2208